Drummer
in
the
Dark 🛜🛜🛜

Other books by Francis Clifford

Drummer in the Dark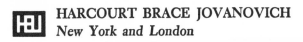

FRANCIS CLIFFORD

HARCOURT BRACE JOVANOVICH
New York and London

Printed in the United States of America

Library of Congress Cataloging in Publication Data

Clifford, Francis.
    Drummer in the dark.

    I. Title.
PZ4.T4666Dr3   [PR6070.H66]   823'.9'14   75-34223
ISBN 0-15-126580-1

B C D E

*For my sons
Peter and Mark*

Drummer in the Dark is a novel.
None of this has taken place
and all the people are imaginary.

"Do not men die fast enough,
without being destroyed by each other?"

—FRANÇOIS DE SALIGNAC DE LA MOTHE FÉNELON

Drummer
in
the
Dark 🛜🛜🛜

 **1**

A wind blew from the east, a cold wind, gusting in from beyond the distant Mourne Mountains, stripping the trees and scattering leaves like slanting brown rain. All week this wind had blown, so that now the trees were almost bare, the look of winter printed across the landscape a month ahead of time.

In other years the shallow valley would still have been rich with the colors of autumn. And the man who sheltered on the ridge would have found thicker cover for himself. As it was he lay in a leaf-filled depression between the roots of some beeches on the forward slope of the hillside, invisible enough even so. The only time he'd expose himself would be when he cut and ran.

Afterwards. Up and away, quick as hell. Everything was in his favor. The border was barely three hundred yards from his position, and he could make that in under a minute; twice he'd done it against the clock.

He was a young man, slim, wiry, with crinkly dark hair and hollows in his cheeks. It was a street-corner face, the grey eyes leaking in the wind, the white nose pinched, the crab-red ears tingling. Under the baggy jacket his shirt was open at the neck, a cloth scarf knotted around his throat. Heavy shoes, worn socks, frayed trousers. And wrists like thin bundles of bone and veins.

He glanced at his watch. It was exactly eleven minutes to three, which meant he'd waited in this place for nearly five hours already; waited and watched. The view he commanded was exceptional, but only the road interested him.

It lay in the trough of the valley like a length of discarded string, green fields and grey rock climbing to either side. Altogether he could see at least a mile of this narrow road, but nothing moved along it. All day nothing had moved, no cars, no people, and a stranger might have concluded the road had been constructed by mistake, or forgotten by the communities it was presumably meant to serve.

The man who kept vigil was not a stranger, though. And he knew that if he waited long enough his patience would be rewarded. He'd wait another day if need be. Two days, three—Jesus, yes. With thin calloused fingers he fumbled in a pocket and pulled out a crumpled pack of Sweet Afton, extracted a cigarette, and ducked his head down towards his right armpit to light up.

Just then he heard the helicopter, only an insect's buzz to begin with, but enough to make his body stiffen. He smashed the cigarette into the earth immediately and searched the sky for something other than scudding streamers of cloud. First the sudden helicopter sweep, then the armored cars along the road. This was what they were doing now. No warning, yet all the warning in the world.

The helicopter's buzz swelled to a snarl. When the man spotted the thing it was banking slightly at about seven or eight hundred feet, and he watched it crisscross the valley, back and forth above the road. He sank down into the leaves and hid his face as the helicopter worked towards him, feeling the air shake as it came thrashing directly over the beech trees, low and threatening, like something searching for him and him alone.

He waited until the zigzag sound of it began to diminish, then surfaced out of the leaves. He was trembling slightly now, though not because of the cold. He poked up his head until he could see the road again, all his attention focused on the point where it emerged from behind a fold in the hillside.

Nothing.

He waited, blinking into the wind, the helicopter's engine beat dying away down valley as swiftly as it had grown, silence flooding back in.

Still nothing.

Minutes passed, every second stretched elastically into doubt-breeding lengths of time. But the man didn't move. Blink, blink—that was all. And trembling a little, as if he had the beginnings of an ague.

Then they came—two Saladins, first one, the other following, the regulation hundred yards between them. They were traveling at about thirty—six-wheeled ten-tonners, compact and deadly; yet from where he lay they looked like models equipped with toy guns. Without taking his eyes away from them, he reached for the small black box half buried in the leaves in front of him and set it on the lip of the depression. Again without looking, by touch alone, he released the trigger locking pin, watching the Saladins as if mesmerized. They were spaced exactly right, the standard gap between them matched by the distance between the two massive charges laid beneath the road four nights earlier. And they had only a quarter of a mile to go before they reached them.

The man was crouching by this time, legs drawn up beneath him. There were two buttons on the box the size of typewriter keys, and his thumbs were positioned over them. He remained absolutely still, oblivious of the bite of the wind, hair flattened, nostrils running, oblivious of everything except the armored cars moving right to left on the curving road and the tiny black-bereted figures of the car commanders standing in their turrets.

Two-fifty yards.

He swallowed, heartbeat pounding in eyes and ears. A bird swooped across his line of vision, but he was blind to it, obsessed, riveted, the seconds rushing away, time and distance narrowing down.

Seventy yards . . . Sixty . . .

5

He sucked in a breath and held it, a last flick-flick with his eyes as he gauged the gap between the cars: it hadn't changed.

Thirty, twenty . . .

Now, he thought.

Viciously he jabbed the buttons down. *Now.* In almost the same instant sections of the road began to crumble, lifting, bulging, taking the Saladins with them through stabbing blossoms of flame. Up and up. From a distance the olive-green cars seemed to be tossed into the air in a dreamlike slow motion, mottled eruptions of earth and stone spurting silently off the valley floor, supporting them, engulfing them.

The man shouted, hands clenched against the sky in exultation. Then the noise reached him, a thunderous double crump, and he started to stumble away, head down, making for the border before the helicopter came flailing back. Against his left side he clutched the small black lethal box. And, as he sprinted for safety, borne on the wind from the very edge of earshot he could hear the sound of someone screaming.

Howard took in what the *Guardian* had to say about it with the expression of somebody who didn't expect to learn anything new. BORDER PATROL AMBUSHED, the headline read; column five, two thirds of the way down. The world was going to hell in several places at one and the same time, so he supposed the *Guardian* had got its front-page balance about right, yet his mouth twitched, as if someone had jabbed him with a needle. Violent death was always an abomination.

"More coffee?"

He grunted and pushed his cup towards his wife.

"What are we doing this evening?"

"I have to see Chisholm."

"Oh?"

"I'm sorry."

"*All* evening?" She gave him a look of bitter hurt. "You aren't dining with him, are you?"

"I am, yes."

"Is it absolutely necessary?"

"I'm afraid so. Weapons Co-ordination is as close to this business as—"

"I do happen to know what Chisholm does."

"Well," he said, "that's why." He eyed her cautiously, part of his mind still occupied with the ambush and its pinpoint accuracy. "I'm sorry, but tonight is Philip's only free evening all week. And we're both in the same boat during the day—chockabloc."

"Damn Weapons Co-ordination."

"Don't say that," he protested mildly.

Her eyes flashed. "Damn everything, then."

Eve was thirty-four, twelve years his junior, and strikingly good-looking; beautiful, even. Far more so than ever Harriet had been, but then, Harriet was an entirely different kind of person in every way. Now, when Howard met other men's wives, quite often he was reminded how extremely fortunate he was; but the trouble with a beautiful face was that after a time you could take it for granted. Habit, and overwork, can win the day.

"How about tomorrow night?" He found an inadequate kind of smile. "We could go to the Diadem, perhaps."

"Tomorrow doesn't matter." Very, very prickly.

"That's childish," he said.

"Thank you."

"You know very well I'm up to my ears." He spread his hands, tired and baffled before he'd even started. Two Saladins lost and nothing to show how it was done. "What's so special about today?"

"It happens to be my birthday." Her timing and tone of voice were crushing.

"Oh God," he heard himself. "It can't be." Then he said: "You're joking. . . . Today?" But even as he floundered into apologies and explanations he knew there wasn't anything he could offer that would do him any good. Of course it was today. *"Qui s'excuse, s'accuse,"* he finished lamely and shrugged, then tried the smile again and wished he hadn't.

How useless words are when they're needed most. He left the second cup of coffee untouched and pushed back his chair; he'd be better off away from the house.

"I have to go," he told her. "All I can say is I'm sorry, truly sorry."

Her cheek was like stone against his lips. "Good-bye, Duncan."

He collected his car coat and swollen brown briefcase and went through to the garage. The white Ford Granada retched a couple of times initially, but the engine was soon as smooth as could be. He drove badly, though, lacking concentration; there was far too much traffic almost from the moment he swung out of the drive on Kingston Hill for his thoughts to be so frequently elsewhere. As a matter of habit he picked up the news at nine, and found the mixture pretty much as before. Soon afterwards, caught by the lights at Putney Bridge and growing impatient, he fumbled Petrie's latest tape from the briefcase and pushed it into the cassette player.

He'd already run it through, last night. And now, as he listened once again, the selfsame sense of distaste fleetingly

8

possessed him. Voyeurs did this. Nobody had a right to such a peepshow, neither he nor Petrie nor anyone else.

"*Tell me something.*"

"*Later.*"

"*Now.*"

"*Later . . . Later.*"

"*When is later?*"

"*Afterwards.*"

"*Who wants afterwards? . . . I want now. . . .*"

Howard's mouth tightened. Every right, he argued, every damn right in the world. Given the circumstances—and he had those with a vengeance.

His office was in Buckingham Gate, and he came the way he'd come a thousand times before—via Parsons Green, through Chelsea, across Eaton Square. One day, he was continually promising himself, he'd explore some other route in the hope of finding an easier journey—though the chances of success were almost nil, and he knew it: London was rapidly becoming a vast thrombotic maze.

"Morning, Mr. Howard."

He left the car for the doorman to park and took the lift up to the third floor. The converted Edwardian mansion was pleasant enough to look at from the outside, but the offices it housed were far from ideal to work in—often too hot in summer, rarely warm enough in winter, nowhere near quiet enough all the year round. Cramped, too, with some of the junior staff practically in each other's laps. But, as the present Minister was forever fond of saying, it was all a matter of purse strings and priorities.

"Morning, sir . . ." "Morning, sir . . ."

Howard pushed into the room marked DIRECTOR and started heaving off his coat. The customary stack of cross-referenced files and interdepartmental memorandums was missing from his desk and, as if to explain the reason why, John Sheard, his personal assistant, knocked and entered almost on his heels.

9

"Jenny's ill, I'm afraid, and won't be in."

"Hell," Howard exclaimed. Jenny Knight was the best secretary he'd ever had. "What's the matter with her?"

"Flu, I believe."

"Today of all days."

He sat down and began emptying his briefcase. Not for the first time he wished to God that the world shortage of paper would start affecting him.

"Anything worth-while?"

"There's another tape from Petrie," Sheard said.

"And . . . ?"

"I haven't got around to it all yet, but Rotterdam's reported back and there's something in from Dublin."

"Constructive?"

"Inconclusive, I'd say. I've only glanced at it, mind."

"Give me what you can, will you?"

"Right away."

Sheard had started for the door when Howard remembered. "How's Carol?"

"Fine."

"When's the baby due?"

"Another couple of weeks."

There was always life. He glanced at Sheard and glimpsed something of his own youth in the fresh-faced eagerness. Go anywhere, do anything—the young hadn't altered much, not really.

"Give me the File Nine stuff from Petrie first."

He played the fresh tape, about six minutes of it altogether, sitting there with his elbows digging into the desk and staring at the photograph taken of Warrick at Galatorsko, warned before he even set the tape running to expect nothing he didn't know already.

Do you think this line's worth pursuing any further? Petrie's covering memo read. *It seems to be getting us absolutely nowhere. . . .*

Howard switched off, deep within himself. Thinking,

thinking. At the present count, there were eighteen files still open, eighteen possibles, and he was going to keep them open, each and every one, even those that instinct already told him would lead elsewhere or finish in dead ends. He took another long hard look at the blown-up print; no doubt about it being Warrick, no doubt about identity at all, no doubt about the place or the time of year. And, because the visual evidence was beyond dispute, this was the file for him, this was where his money had been for weeks and still remained.

Yes. Despite the setbacks and frustrations. *Yes.* File Nine.

His eye spotted the reminder stuck in the corner of his blotter: *Chisholm, Fisher's 7:30.* And immediately he was alerted to do something else; incredibly, it had slipped his mind a second time. Already. With a stab of guilt he buzzed Sheard and asked him to arrange for flowers to be sent to Eve. Jenny would have coped without another word, but Sheard wanted chapter and verse.

"What sort of flowers, sir?"

"Two dozen roses."

"They do them in tens now, I believe."

"Tens, then. Two tens."

"Red roses?"

"Red roses, yes."

"With a message?"

"Yes," Howard said. The other phone began to ring just then and he hesitated, wondering if it was the Minister about the ambush south of Crossmaglen. Tethered by the thought he muttered absently to Sheard what he wanted on the card. "Just say: Love, Duncan."

11

In the early days, Leach was apt to screw up parking the mobile unit a good three times out of four: he found it too damned long, for one thing. But ham-fisted miscalculations were over and done with since quite a while back and he'd completely mastered the way of it now, space to play with or no.

It was dead on three o'clock when he first glimpsed the massive spire of the Palace of Culture above the blur of Warsaw's skyline. He was heading northeast on the road in from Lodz, flanked by the ironed-out distances that stretched interminably to either side, the road good and a cold-looking sun behind him. And from then on the spire was like an aiming mark. Barely twenty minutes later he had brought the heavy articulated vehicle neatly to rest outside the towering Forum Hotel in the city's center, and well before he'd eased himself from behind the wheel, the curious were gathering to stare.

"Isn't that—in part, at least—the object of the exercise?" Sir Gordon Saxon used to argue. "Let 'em see you're coming, let 'em know you're there."

Emblazoned along its sixty-foot length the silver unit bore the royal-blue legend SAXON ENGINEERING. Beneath this, in English, French, and German was painted MOBILE TRADE DISPLAY. Large detachable scarlet stickers temporarily repeated the information in Polish. If Sir Gordon was right about nothing else, he was right about the vehicle's visual impact; at the very least it turned people's heads. But although this succeeded in making the name of Saxon better and more internationally known among the public at large, the prime function of the unit was to exhibit to potential customers as wide a range of Saxon products as possible.

"Come on in," Leach's invitation always was, "and see what's in our shop window." In less than two years he'd opened up quite substantial markets in Hungary, Czechoslovakia, Poland, and East Germany, the novelty of the mobile display as much a factor as his own no-nonsense style of salesmanship. At thirty-one he was something of a Jack-of-all-trades—fluent in two foreign languages, grounded in basic engineering, licensed to handle heavy vehicles; on top of which there was room inside the unit for him to project selected films to a seated audience of twelve. Back at the company's London headquarters in Kingsway, Saxon Engineering was proudly aware it had got itself a winning combination.

Leach took his bag from the driving cab and went through the big frameless glass entrance into the hotel's cavernous foyer, people coming and going all the time, the tourist season over and done with yet plenty of human traffic all the same—Japanese, Germans, Arabs, Swedes; he wasn't alone in having put a foot into a widening trade door. He smiled at the striking blonde in Reception, and told her he had a reservation.

"Your name, please?"

"Martin Leach."

Every month for the past year and a half he'd had a four- or five-day booking at the Forum, and by now he recognized many of the faces across the desk. Not here, though. The girl checked the records, bending forward with arms crossed, elbows cupped in her hands. Room 448, she told him with a nod and quick smile of her own. Leach thanked her, then completed the registration card and relinquished his passport, after which he rode up in the lift, no one else with him, and walked the corridor to his room, where the obedient color matchings almost convinced him for a moment that he'd been in there before.

He tossed his bag on the bed before crossing to the window. Only someone who had lived through it all could have heard the echoes of Warsaw's terrible past as he looked down on Marszalkowska Street and its clean-cut surroundings; Leach was too young for that, and, in any case, he lacked the imagination. The inner grid of the modern city he knew consisted in the main of multistory office and apartment blocks, vast streets, heroic monuments, a surprising number of restored churches, and a few small parks and gardens, their public benches deserted now, the plane trees bare and leprous-looking.

Below, a trolley clanked by and the sidewalks were crowded. Leach yawned silently and lit a cigarette, the pale ghost of his own reflection visible in the glass—flat ears, narrow nose, firm mouth, thick dark hair. After a short while he turned away. On an impulse he reached for the telephone, lifted it, heard the operator saying "Yes? . . . Yes?", then suddenly changed his mind and hung up.

Whistling, he started to undress, padding back and forth into the bathroom. When he'd showered and dried himself, he got into some fresh clothes, emptied his bag of everything except essentials, and left the room. It was ten past four by this time. Downstairs, in the telephone bay in the far corner of the foyer, he found an empty booth and called Anna Dabrowska.

She didn't keep him waiting long. Polish was beyond him, but he supposed she said: "Who is it?" Something like that. "Who's there?"

"A friend," he answered.

She gave a little squeal and changed to English. "I thought you wouldn't be here until later. Some time tonight."

"I left early."

"Where did you leave?"

"Lodz."

"What were you doing in Lodz?" So precise always.

"Selling things to your textile industry."

"Successfully?"

"Ask me again this time next year." Leach chuckled. "How've you been?"

"Come and find out."

"Now?"

"Why not?"

"Are you finished for the day?"

"I'm at home, aren't I?"

"Sure," he said and laughed again. "Ten minutes, then. Fifteen, maybe. Depends on how the taxis are."

"Okay."

"See you, Anna."

He hung up but didn't leave the booth. Instead, he fished in his pocket for another coin. For several seconds he stood with eyes closed and lips pressed tight as he summoned Retman's number from his memory. Then he dialed—nothing ever written down, as little as possible ever done that might provide a culture for suspicion.

"Marek Retman."

"I've just got in," Leach told him in German, "and I'm staying five days."

That was all.

Sunset smothered the day and dark came.

Howard remained at Buckingham Gate until after everyone else had gone. It was seven before he let himself out of the office and put the locks on. He walked to where the car was parked, glad of his coat, a bite in the November air, and drove to Soho through the gaudy streets, crowded now and neon-bright.

He liked Fisher's. For years it had been the place that first came to mind when he wanted a working lunch or dinner. No one sat elbow to elbow or was squeezed in back to back. There was room to move, room to talk. Eve didn't care for it—too damned dull, she said it was, and she maybe had a point. But it sometimes suited his purpose, and the food was always excellent, the service friendly and discreet.

He arrived a good ten minutes before Chisholm and went to the bar.

"Scotch, please. A large Bell's . . . with ice and water."

Weapons Co-ordination was in Northumberland Avenue, and he reckoned Chisholm would come on foot. Fitness fanatic, Chisholm was, running across Hyde Park each morning and doing daily press-ups in the office.

Incredible. But he had an iron-hard look to show for it and a sharp mind to match. If Howard found himself in similar shape in his middle fifties, he knew he'd be as astonished as he would be grateful.

He badly needed the whiskey. He felt drained, sick of questions without answers, weary of trying to juggle with more than he knew how. There had been too many false hopes, too many blind alleys, above all, too many deaths. For months past. And now there was a newcomer to contend with, now—on top of everything—there was Touchbutton.

Restlessly he glanced at the public image of himself in the tinted glass behind the bar and fingered his neck. Museum exhibit, what people saw—decent clothes, squarish face, sandy-brown hair, a hint of pallor beneath the summer's fading tan.

"D'you happen to have a light?"

He turned to the woman on the nearby stool, the only other person there—thirty-fiveish and plump and almost

16

pretty, a cigarette held provocatively close to her smiling lips.

"Sorry." He shook his head. "I don't smoke."

The lean Italian barman came to her rescue. Their hands made contact as the match flared, and the woman didn't move hers away, Howard noticed. Unexpectedly he thought of Eve, his mind dragged from its consuming obsession, and for a brief moment all he was aware of was a sort of emptiness that seemed to carry within it the seeds of some unknown future pain.

Then Chisholm arrived. "Hello," he said from behind. "Been waiting long?"

"Hello, Philip . . . No. Beat you by a head, that's all. What'll it be?"

"A pink, please."

Chisholm perched alongside. He had the darkest eyes Howard had ever known, the irises almost black, and his mouth was like a wound.

"How's it been?"

Howard's shrug was an answer in itself.

"You, too? I spent most of the day with politicians."

"God help you."

"Last year's words and last year's language," Chisholm grunted. "God help us all."

He raised his glass. "Cheers." Big hands, wide shoulders, as tough as nails. And wonderfully reliable. "How's Eve?"

"Fine," Howard said, hiding himself away. "Oh, she's fine. . . . Sent her love."

Close by, the woman laughed at something the barman was telling her. "Why?" she asked. "How do you know? . . . I should like proof of that." She lowered her voice and laughed again. "I don't believe a word of it. . . ."

Chisholm shot her a glance, as if surprised to find that he and Howard weren't alone, then turned his back on her. "There's been another one—did you hear?"

"When?"

"Within the last hour. Someone told me the BBC interrupted programs with a news flash."

"Bad?"

"A monster, apparently. Near Liverpool. They'll be ramming them down our throats next." Chisholm drained his glass, trapping the ice with his teeth. "Want the other half? Or shall we go and eat?"

"Let's eat," Howard said with sudden impatience. They went through into the restaurant and were guided to the corner table Howard generally occupied.

"Good evening, Mr. Howard. Nice to see you again. . . ." He acknowledged the greeting distantly, without warmth. There was a war on and he was losing it. Things were getting worse, worse every day. The waiter fussed around, adjusting the place settings, changing the blood-red lampshade's rake, finally leaving them with a large crisp parchment menu each.

And Howard said: "Many casualties?"

"Seems so."

"Where'd it happen?"

"Railway station. As I say, I only got it secondhand, so I don't know which. Nor do I know whether there's been a Touchbutton claim or not."

There had been three claims so far. "This is Touchbutton. . . . Touchbutton, right?" The same soft brogue each time. "We took the Saladins today"—that was the style of it. No more, no less, a single phone call to the nearest army post, finished and done with before there was any chance of being traced.

Touchbutton . . . Not all that long ago no one had so much as heard the name.

"Somehow I doubt it," Chisholm added as an afterthought.

"Why?"

"Doesn't strike me as being selective enough. One of

two things the Touchbutton incidents have all had in common is that they've picked off their targets like a sniper. This thing tonight sounds like the usual random holocaust."

"There could have been a train passing through," Howard pointed out.

Chisholm ignored that. "Take 'em in order." He began ticking off his fingers. "Judge Walsh—right? Out walking his dog. What happens? Tree stump explodes the moment he's alongside. It's my belief that one was in the nature of a trial, an experiment, if you like, using a small charge and detonating it from fairly close range. Whether I'm right or wrong doesn't much matter: what does is that Walsh was a moving target when they blew him to kingdom come. And so was the ferryboat, Touchbutton number two —that was a moving target, all right, and it went up when it was in mid-channel with a full load of troops and their families. And then the Saladins—thirty miles an hour and Touchbutton singled them out to the split second."

Howard beckoned to their waiter, and for a short while they concentrated on what they would eat, fairly brisk about it, no leisurely savoring of alternatives. Potted shrimps and veal escalope, avocado vinaigrette and steak au poivre— the distraction of choosing didn't take long.

"What wine, Mr. Howard?"

"Let's have a carafe of red. . . . All right, Philip? Suit you?"

"Sure," Chisholm agreed, not really listening. He lit a cigarette, and the smoke curled lazily around the lamp.

Howard waited a little while. "What's the second thing Touchbuttons have in common?"

"Method of detonation."

"Ah, yes."

"To my mind it's already as good as proved they're activated by radio signal." Chisholm spread his hands and arched his thick eyebrows as if anticipating opposition.

"How flaming else? There's no other way in the light of the evidence. All three were too bull's-eye exact to have been fired by normal timing mechanisms. Quite impossible . . . And in the absence of any wiring in the vicinity of the target area it can only mean they've got possession of something pretty special. *And* expensive—though I doubt if they have to count that kind of cost. . . . Any straws in the wind about where they could have been shopping?"

"I don't even know what we're looking for yet."

"Where do they usually go?"

"Libya . . . East Germany . . ." Howard creased his forehead. "They've never been choosy. North Korea's done them a turn or two in the past." He took a long slow wincing breath. "We're sure about so little, so bloody little. . . . And I don't mind admitting that Touchbutton's potential scares me stiff. All of a sudden my feeling is that what we've seen of it so far is just the beginning of something much more terrible."

"They still have to plant the charges—whoever they are. So they still run the same risks as with conventional—"

"Agreed. But once that's done, and by whatever means it's done, then it seems to me they've got it made. They can bide their time and start their countdown when they want." Howard glanced sidelong at Chisholm. "We're in for precision bombing. If you're right, that is, and they *are* using detonators activated by radio signal."

"What else?"

"You're the expert."

"I'm right," Chisholm said firmly. "And I daresay you're right, too. In which case things'll get a damned sight worse before they start getting any better."

 **5**

Anna Dabrowska's small apartment was a couple of hundred meters at most from the Vistula's left bank and roughly the same distance to the north of the Poniatowski bridge. Spaced round and about were other lofty apartment blocks, risen from the ruins like nearly everything else in sight, while almost opposite, across the busy wide brown river, was the huge stadium the crowds flocked to throughout most of the year and where Leach was once upon a time forever telling himself he really ought to go to kill a couple of hours or more.

He was lonely then, with few contacts and no friends, trying to adjust to a new country every few days, knowing a little about too many places and not enough about anywhere in particular. Months passed for him in a state of near isolation, and during this period he reported back to London without any great enthusiasm for his prospects. But gradually things started to improve. He made headway, slow but sure. The mobile trade-display unit no longer seemed a wasteful white elephant that aroused initial curiosity and nothing much else. In Budapest and Prague and Warsaw and Berlin and elsewhere he began to be greeted by familiar faces, voices, handshakes. As far as Saxon Engineering was concerned, within a year of first starting out behind the wheel of the trailer, his efforts had more than paid off. But it wasn't until he met Anna by chance that his personal loneliness came to an end.

Four months ago, in the Old Town, at one of the Ruch shops in the market square, Anna stepped into his life when he was in difficulties over some postcards he was buying. "Can I help you, please?" As simple as that.

Afterwards, with pigeons clap-clapping into flight off

the sun-drenched cobbles, Leach thanked her again, complimenting her on her English.

"You are very kind—but it is not so difficult for me. I studied English at the university."

"In Poland," he joked, "I reckon someone like me needs someone like you right here in his pocket."

Attractive though she was, he was on the point of letting her go; strangers often came to the rescue. But she said: "You have other problems?" With such a smile.

"I haven't done all my shopping, if that's what you mean."

Two days later he went to her apartment for the first time and made love to her there. Anna Dabrowska. She moved behind him and covered his face with her slim hands and breathed a laugh almost into his right ear, teasing, like a child playing games.

"No looking."

He stood obediently in the darkness of his own making, pulse quickening as he listened to the rustle and slide of her clothes coming off.

"Turn around."

He obeyed, scarcely believing the way it was happening, never like this with anyone before. Seconds passed without a sound, his imagination cutting loose, and it seemed like a year's wait at the one still point of the turning world.

"Now you can open your eyes," she said at last.

And so it began for him, the heat of summer saturating the sprawling city and no thought in his mind about tomorrow.

It was the simplest of apartments: a few framed prints on the color-washed walls, plenty of sturdy dark furniture, some potted cacti by the windows, no photographs, no television, cream lampshades with rusted fringes on them.

"Happy?" Anna asked now, an hour after he'd arrived from the Forum.

"You bet."

"How many days will you stay?"

"Until Friday."

She groaned. "No longer?"

" 'Fraid not."

"Each time it is the same. Always the same."

"I know."

"So what are you doing about it?" Raven-black hair strewn over the pillow and green eyes trembling, green on white. "Tell me that."

"I hate not being here."

"Do you say that to some girl in Prague as well?"

"There is no girl in Prague."

"Budapest, then."

"There's only you, Anna."

"No one in London?"

"You know damned well."

"A wife, perhaps?"

"No wife . . . Nobody."

He smiled at her, tracing the shape of her lips with a finger. How little they still knew about each other. All he could swear to was the wildness he was able to unleash, kisses with dreams in them, the look and the feel of her. Four months, and in some respects they hadn't really started.

She was twenty-five and she worked in a printing house; that much he'd learned. She had gone there soon after leaving Cracow University, and somewhere along the way he seemed to remember her telling him she was employed as a secretary; he didn't bother himself with the details. Cracow was where she came from, but there was no family home any more: both her parents were dead, killed four years ago in a head-on car crash, and the only living relative she ever spoke of was an older sister, now in America. This sister's name was Krystyna, and when Anna mentioned her the references were invariably both envious and accusing.

Small wonder. Krystyna had visited America on a stu-

23

dent's passport and turned her back on Poland while she was there. Now she was in Springfield, Ohio, and everything was just fine, thank you. But because of her defection Anna would never be able to obtain a passport for herself.

"Never?"

"Never."

"But surely—"

"Martin, Martin . . . How little you know."

She was bitter about it. The only times Leach had seen her angry or resentful was when she spoke of what her sister had done, and what it had cost in terms of her own freedom. "Listen," she had told him, paraphrasing official dogma. The state invested in the education and training of each individual, and if that investment was squandered by any one person, the state took steps to ensure that other members of that family were not allowed the same temptations. Every man and woman in the country was aware of the rules, and all but a small minority accepted them.

"Not Anna Dabrowska, though."

"Haven't I good reason?" she'd countered. "How would you like it if they told you in London that you could never leave England?"

"I wouldn't, naturally."

"Of course you wouldn't, you, of all people. . . . Imagine it."

Every few weeks Leach arrived in Warsaw. And from the moment he got in they were together as much as possible, hungry for each other. Sometimes in the summer evenings they had sauntered by the river or in one of the smaller parks, red squirrels among the chestnut trees and the cobweb touch of her hair against his cheek as they walked. Now and again they went to eat in an out-of-the-way restaurant suggested by Anna; once or twice they danced. They were very special days for both of them, unreal, in a way, and never perfect, haunted throughout by the sense of impermanence.

And in between Leach earned his keep.

Two things she had asked of him. First, that he never call for her at the office. Second, that she didn't have to join him at the hotel.

"Does it worry you?"

"How d'you mean?"

"My asking things of you. Special things like that."

"No," he'd said. "Of course not."

She knew best. Some places were more in the public eye than others, and it made sense to be discreet. Discretion was part of his own survival kit, and he went willingly along with what she wanted. A lot of the time they kept themselves to themselves, lovers, as now, so often as now, the tips of her breasts like big pink blotches and the room all shapes and shades of shadow.

She kissed him, soft against him, sighing. "What's to become of us, Martin?"

"I don't ask that sort of question."

"You would if the answer was important to you."

"It's important."

"How can it be?"

"It's important," he insisted.

He'd never felt this way. There had been a succession of women, moments galore when there was no before or after, good times in half a dozen countries. But no chords ever struck, nothing touched that went deeper than the skin. And eventually, without fail, all they'd ever led him to were lies and recriminations—theirs and his own. Sooner or later it always came to that.

Love? He didn't know what it meant or what it might demand. In his parents' semidetached house in Bromley it was never given a chance, a language never practiced and so allowed to die. "Love's a bloody cheat and a fraud" was one of the things his mother so often used to say, and as that was after his librarian father had abandoned them for a giggling brunette only half his age it wasn't as though his mother hadn't cause to be bitter; good cause. But bitterness and endless harking back make no kind of sense to the young, and Leach was young then—fourteen, to be exact. Fourteen, no brother, no sisters. He took the brunt for a couple of years, then quit himself, walked out, went up to London, scraped and saved and survived, acquiring a taste for money along the way, a weakness for it.

Love? Almost without his being aware of what was happening, time and chance had brought him to a door that was opening onto another kind of future, and he wasn't able to discuss it as if it were already a reality.

Not yet anyway. He'd never learned how.

And, besides, there were complications—Retman being one, Retman who paid so well.

"Tell me," Anna said. "What are we doing tonight?" It was getting on toward nine o'clock.

"You're the boss."

She drew her lips into a faintly sardonic grimace of rebuke. "Never that." And then, with sudden feeling, she exclaimed: "If only I could come with you, go away from here."

"How?" he was about to say. "How could that be done?" But she moved against him and desire returned, nailing them.

 **6**

The phone booth windows were steamed up and the man couldn't see outside. ALL BRITISH ARE MUCK was scrawled in lipstick across the glass-covered dialing instructions, the first word viciously underlined.

"Listen."

He scarcely moved his lips and kept his voice low.

"Try number fourteen Kilbrennan Street." The flat muffled vowels came from the very back of the throat. "If it's weapons you're wanting, then the journey won't be wasted."

"Who is this?"

"Did you hear me?" the man said. "Fourteen Kilbrennan Street."

"I've got it."

"Under the floor in the downstairs front room."

"Right."

"Number fourteen . . . Be sure it's number fourteen."

"Got it," the duty corporal said again. "Who is this?" But a dribbling sound was in his left ear and suddenly he was talking to himself. "Shit," he muttered.

He slammed the phone down and picked up the one beside it.

"Coporal Rixon here, sir."

"Yes?"

"Anonymous tip-off about a possible arms cache. One four Kilbrennan Street. Special reference to floor in downstairs front room."

He logged the call as he spoke, squinting up at the clock above his head and timing it as having come in at exactly 2112.

The captain studied the street map for longer than was necessary merely to locate the whereabouts of the house.

Sometimes they had this kind of call a couple of times or so in a week and it could mean anything.

Ambush, as like as not. Booby trap, false alarm. Anything . . . Only last month one of his men had stepped through an open door straight into the obituary columns.

"Why should they want to turn each other in?" the sergeant at his elbow said, frowning, fresh from a stint at the training depot, where comradeship was the creed of every recruit. "For what reason?"

"Don't ask me."

"It's got to be something else. What makes one of the bastards go to a phone and—?"

"Perhaps," the captain said, "someone's been screwing his sister."

"Even so."

"Perhaps is the name of the game, Sergeant."

Number fourteen was the end house on Kilbrennan Street. The street itself was one of many that branched away from others like it and then, in turn, sprouted mean-faced alleys and cul-de-sacs of its own. At the best of times it must have been an awful place in which to live, ugly and comfortless, soiled by decades of poverty and industrial grime—and the best of times had long since gone. Joy was a word here; suspicion and hatred the stark realities, sudden death as well. There were children of school age now who had never known anything else except variations of this selfsame nightmare.

In his mind's eye the captain pictured the cross of grey tarmac at the street intersection near the house, the narrow sidewalks leading directly past windows and front doors, all the labyrinthine ways of approach and withdrawal. This was no man's land, neither hard-core Catholic nor Protestant, republican nor loyalist. But no less dangerous because of that.

He went on looking at the street layout for perhaps a whole minute more. Then, very methodically, he began to indicate exactly how the raid squad was to be deployed, crispness in his voice as his fingers spidered over the map, stressing a detail here, a field of fire there. Finally he pointed to the walled yard shown at the back of the house.

"Cover the rear, Sergeant. You and one."

"Sir."

"And be ready to move at 2200."

They quit the armored personnel carrier a couple of street lengths from their objective—ten of them in the squad, faces smeared black, rifles chest high and at the ready. Rain was falling vertically, the air sullen and still. They moved fast, spread out, silent in rubber-soled boots. A stray dog yapped at them from the shored-up ruins of a fire-bombed pub, a pair of old men stopped uncertainly in their tracks and watched them pass, an unseen woman screamed from the shadows as they ran—"Pigs, pigs, fucking pigs."

Incredibly, this was a part of the United Kingdom.

They closed on number fourteen, pad-pad-pad along the sidewalk, street-lamp reflections shimmering in the wet. No tall buildings hemmed them in, nothing above two stories high, yet there were vantage points in plenty for any waiting marksman. And here, as they crossed the intersection, they were absurdly vulnerable, a total absence of traffic, the silence like something lying in ambush.

"Lights!"

Two of the squad shot out the overhead lamps, seven shots in quick succession, the sound of each crack and explosion ricocheting from wall to wall and away. A cloak of semidarkness dropped over them as they sprinted into position, separating, the rear of the house soon covered, four street corners manned, the captain and two others at number fourteen's door.

"Open up!" Thump, thump with a pistol butt. "Open up!"

In house after house along Kilbrennan Street lights were being frantically switched off.

"Open up!"

Nothing from upstairs or down. Not a glimmer from inside.

"Twenty seconds, then we come in," the captain warned, loud and clear.

He licked his lips, suddenly dry despite the rain. Still no response.

"Five..."

He waited, wire taut, sideways to the door. Empty houses were always sods.

"Ten..."

He moved six paces along the narrow sidewalk to the only ground-floor window. Heavy curtains were drawn across it, as good as a blindfold. *Fourteen Kilbrennan Street. Special reference to downstairs front room* . . .

"Fifteen seconds," he barked.

Nothing. Nothing but the quiet in the street, like a huge conspiracy. He signaled with his head to the two men with him.

"Cover me."

Window catches could be fatal if they'd been tampered with; so could window ledges, window frames. . . . But he'd rather chance the window than risk the door.

"Twenty . . ."

So be it. The captain took a deep breath and began smashing the glass.

 **7**

Chisholm lived north of the river and was well served by the tube.

"Keep smiling," he said to Howard as they were leaving Fisher's. "You're bound to get a lead eventually."

"Want to bet?"

"You always have in the past."

"That doesn't exactly provide a guarantee."

"Come on," Chisholm chided. "If I didn't know you, I'd say you sounded like throwing in the towel."

"But since you know me—?"

"I'd say you're tired."

"Punch drunk?"

"Tired."

"Good night, Philip." Howard touched the older man's sleeve. "Safe home now."

"You, too."

He walked past the strip clubs to the all-night car park on the other side of Shaftesbury Avenue. At one of the corners on the way he paused momentarily, and a lurking pimp misread the hesitation.

"Looking for something special?" Suddenly as close as a pickpocket. "Extra special?"

"Push off."

Sunken cheeks and dead eyes. "Just tell me what you've got in mind."

"*Push off.*"

So much of the world was sick. Howard found his way to where he'd left the Granada and began the journey home. The 11:30 news from L.B.C. was dominated by the Liverpool bomb—seventeen dead and fifty or so mutilated. "Shortly after the explosion an anonymous caller telephoned a local newspaper and made the now familiar Touchbutton claim. . . ."

Howard stiffened at the wheel. All evening he had sensed that Chisholm's guess was wrong. This *was* number four, Touchbutton number four, and he'd almost been prepared to hear it said. And yet, as he listened, he felt as if something had crawled into his guts and begun to fester there.

On a good night he could get to Kingston Hill in well under a half hour, but this wasn't one of them. Most of the signals were against him and there was a four-car pile-up in Knightsbridge, which didn't help, the long backup making chaos at Hyde Park Corner. Even so, he was able to nose into the garage alongside Eve's Mini only a little after midnight, his body too taut to relax when the engine died, the sensation of movement still with him as he entered the house.

How quiet it was, the worlds overlapping. Lights were on everywhere, and he went around switching most of them off before going upstairs. The roses Sheard had undertaken to have delivered were in the hall, and Howard thought they already looked faded, the arrangement sloppily indifferent, as if done in pique. But at least they prodded his memory.

He was quite sure Eve would still be awake—reading, most likely—so it came as a surprise to find her fast asleep. He stood for a moment with the door not closed, touched by a pang of guilt and regret at what he saw. It seemed hard on her suddenly, curled up there alone after a birthday evening spent by herself.

"Eve?"

She didn't stir. On the pillow her face had a great calmness, with none of the morning's dissatisfaction. But early to bed wasn't part of her scheme of things at all, and the thought crossed his mind that she might have wanted to rub salt in the wound by having him find her like this; even taken a Mogadon to make sure.

All the same, he thought, silently shutting the door, *mea culpa.*

Propped against the alarm clock there was a note. *Colin rang*—that was all; just the two scrawled words on a used envelope. No mention of what about or whether he would call again or whether he expected to be called back. So the matter wasn't urgent; Eve would have said so otherwise. Which meant it could wait until morning.

Howard yawned and began to undress. He was in bed ten minutes later, restless from the start, black coffee the culprit, as so often before. For what seemed an interminable stretch of time he traipsed over everything Chisholm had said, back and forth, as if repetition might unearth something different, and when he'd done with that he found himself grasshopping around between the disappointing contents of Petrie's tapes and the latest casualty figures and the concern the Home Secretary was privately beginning to express, clichés and all, about things hanging by a thread and the security forces losing the upper hand, et cetera.

Only in sleep was there any escape, and he achieved it eventually. A dream took him under, the first dream that comes with the first sleep, and for some reason he found himself at Mass with Harriet. Colin wasn't with them—which he might well have been, as either a child or a teenager—and Howard couldn't make out which church they were in. Nothing was sharp-edged, nothing too clear, not even the corpse stretched on the cross. "All that love and pain," Harriet said to him. And in the dream Howard knew that none of this belonged here and now. Harriet was dead, and he didn't go to churches any more. Yet the phrase was real enough, straight out of what used to be, and he made a small sound, like a cry, as he remembered

33

how happy they had always been and Harriet's way of touching people as if she loved them.

The dream abandoned him and he passed into oblivion. God knows for how long; he went deep, deep down. Then something started drilling into his brain, blunt and insistent.

Burp, burp . . .

Colin. He was clutching at last things as he surfaced. It was sure to be Colin.

Burp, burp . . .

"Oh, damn," Eve started. "Oh, *damn.*"

Howard fumbled the phone off the rest. "Duncan?" someone was saying excitedly as he put the thing to his ear. Not Colin, whoever it was.

"Howard speaking."

"Philip here, Duncan."

He still didn't recognize him. "Who?" he said stupidly, his own voice thick and rasping.

"Philip Chisholm . . . Listen—"

"Philip?" Wits resurrecting, lying there in the darkness. "Sorry, I'm—"

"Listen . . . I think we're on to something."

"I'm not with you."

"What does he want, for Christ's sake?"—Eve.

"We think we've got a Touchbutton," Chisholm was saying.

"No!"

"Sounds very much like it."

"God in heaven." Howard jerked into a sitting position and snapped on the light. "Say that again."

"There was a tip-off, apparently. Out of the blue."

"Where?"

"Belfast."

"When'd this happen?"

"Tonight. Hours ago."

"God in heaven," Howard repeated.

The clock was showing twenty-five to five. His mind was beginning to pick up speed, and questions were forming, questions galore, and all the time Chisholm was jabbering nonstop.

"How d'you know it's a Touchbutton?" Howard cut in. "How *can* you know? . . . Is it labeled or something?"

"I've been given a description."

"Yes?"

"The senior A.T.O. in the area says that what they've taken possession of is a control handset and what they suspect are radio-activated detonators."

"How big's the handset?"

"Six by four by three—that kind of thing. 'Bout the size of a small cassette player. Seems that it's boxed with its own complementary detonator supply."

Howard snorted. "Gift-wrapped."

"After a fashion."

"Any clue as to who's doing the giving?"

"That I couldn't say." Chisholm's voice was half an octave higher than normal. "Isn't it fantastic, though? The very thing Weapons Co-ordination's been praying for."

"Seeing's believing."

"Oh, sure . . . But it sounds exactly the kind of device I was suggesting, and I can't believe—"

"Not too small? Could something that size transmit a sufficiently strong signal?"

"Over a limited range. I don't see why not."

The line spat at them both. "You going up there?"

"Nine o'clock, Heathrow. Come and have a look at what sort of toy we've laid our hands on."

"I can't," Howard said. "I'm caught up with the Home Secretary in the morning. But I'd like to have one of my people keep you company."

"Fine."

"John Sheard—I think you know him."

35

"I do, yes."

"I'll get on to him right away. And I'll have my fingers crossed for you."

"For us all, Duncan . . . Incidentally, I was wrong about Liverpool."

"I know. I heard."

"Bastards, aren't they?" Then: "Apologies to Eve for disturbing her beauty sleep."

"Sure."

Howard cut off and dialed Sheard's number immediately, wide awake now. All Sheard wanted to know was how long he would be gone. "Twenty-four hours?" Howard suggested. With Carol the way she was, he supposed Sheard's reaction was almost inevitable. "As soon as Chisholm's run a few range tests he'll be anxious to wing his way straight home."

He lay back, no more sleep after this. A degree of Chisholm's excitement had brushed off, but he needed a sounding board for doubts and reservations. It was necessary for him to talk, not merely to explain.

"We've had some good luck for a change," he began, thoughts tugging in different directions. "And not before time."

Eve shifted lazily, closer. "What part of the night is it?"

"Quarter to five." Somewhere on the surface of his feelings he was aware of being disappointed that she didn't ask what kind of good luck it was. "Philip asked your forgiveness."

"So I should think," she said, the anger gone out of her voice.

"Always such an optimist, that man. I hope to God he hasn't put two and two together and made five."

Just the clock ticking; nothing but that for a while. And Howard all nerves, as strained as hell.

Eve said: "Was I asleep when you got in?"

"That's right."

"When was that?"

"Around midnight."

He gazed up at the splash of lamplight on the ceiling. A change of luck, yes. But, on reflection, nothing to go overboard about. Even if Chisholm returned triumphant with a Touchbutton, and Weapons Co-ordination circulated a mass of data to all and sundry, how did it help if no one could say who supplied the things and how they got to where they did the damage?

His mouth twitched. "We're still at square one," he thought aloud. "Until we know where they got them from we're as good as marking time."

They, he thought, and hated them in the plural.

Eve slid an arm behind his neck. "Deserter," she said.

"When?" he queried absently.

"On my birthday." She kissed his face, shaping her body against his. But nothing moved in him.

"Did you know Touchbutton claimed responsibility for this Liverpool bomb?"

She didn't answer, didn't hear.

"Okay, Philip's maybe going to have a sample under his belt. But I'm no nearer to what I want than I was at the beginning. And what good's the one without the other? We need to know who as well as how."

"Duncan," Eve whispered.

The ghosts of the smashed and drowned children on the ferryboat took over the cornerstones of his mind. He had never realized that pity could flip a coin that came down hate side up. There were eighteen files still open at the office, each and every one a searching after revenge: that's what it amounted to. And so far he'd got nowhere. Touchbutton number four and he'd got nowhere.

"Duncan . . . For God's sake . . ."

Nothing moved in him. He could feel the thud of

Eve's heart and the drag of her fingers on his skin and the soft insistence of her lips, but it was like something happening to someone else. All of it.

"Please."

He pressed his nails into the palms of his hands so that pain might stop his mind from running away. There wasn't a part of Eve he didn't know or a way of her loving him he hadn't experienced. But all she stirred in him was despair. He seemed numb, dead on the surface as well as at the core.

"I'm sorry. . . . Sorry."

"What's happened to you?"

"I'm sorry."

"Oh Christ," she said, teeth clenched.

"It's no good."

She jerked away and lay still, leaden. They heard the insistent tick-tick-tick of the clock again, their minds prickling. A long time seemed to pass, measured off into fractions.

"You should see a doctor," Eve said at last, heavy with resignation.

"That's ridiculous."

"You can't go on like this." She delayed fractionally. "Well, maybe *you* can. But I can't. . . . You just aren't there any more."

Howard's voice shook. "Listen," he began.

"What's the use? It's not just this. It's in every way. I've been pushed into the background of your life somehow, and it can't go on."

Howard closed his eyes, afraid of the truth of what she was saying, afraid of failure, defensive and edgy and close to despair.

"I can't stand it," Eve said. "And I don't see why I should."

He said lamely: "I've got a load on my mind, Eve."

"So've I. Jesus Christ, so have I."

"This whole bloody business has suddenly come a lot nearer home. And we're hardly any further—"

"This is home," Eve said, "and the whole bloody business, as you put it, has been here for weeks. Right inside the door. It's had the run of the house and I've been living with it."

"I can't work nine to five," he protested. "It's not that kind of job and never was. You know damn well. This job of mine eats you. It chews you up and it spits you out."

"Other people in the department manage. Other marriages don't shrivel up and die."

"Don't say that."

"Why not, if it's true?"

They were silent then, lost within themselves, a barrier between them. Hurt and indignant and alarmed they watched the curtains lighten as the night slowly drained away, and with the dawn there came the small sound of birds and the beginning of another morning.

When Howard finally found his tongue again he asked: "What did Colin want?"

"He said he'll call you at the office."

There were no birds here, and never had been. Only a floor and a wall, and a man's body arched between the two.

"On your toes, MacAlindon," the corporal barked. Cropped head, cropped mind. "Up on your bleeding toes."

A naked bulb hung on a length of cord, and the corporal's shadow moved back and forth, back and forth. The man's shoes were off and he wore no jacket. Behind him, well away from the wall, a stocky Intelligence Corps major sat at a baize-topped table reading a book. He looked bored and in need of sleep.

"Rack your brains, MacAlindon . . . *Think!*"

Six hours this had lasted. Six hours since the man had been hustled from Kilbrennan Street to wherever he was now and made to support himself in this fashion—heels not touching the floor and splayed finger tips against the wall. Six hours without respite. To begin with, when he was at little more than arm's length from the wall, the position was tolerable enough. His brain was clear then and his muscles were strong and his will was stubbornly intact.

Not any more, though.

"Gone deaf have you, MacAlindon?"

He was a big man, around six feet and strongly built. Thirty-ish. Both forearms were lightly tattooed, and his dark hair was thick and wild with waves. Throughout the first hour his arms had been as steady as buttresses and his head had stayed high. And not a single word had come out of him.

"Deaf, are you?"

He groaned now. His head was slumped and his arms and legs trembled and his nerve ends everywhere shrieked with pain. Below the arch he had made of himself the stone floor was spattered with sweat, and the stink of his suffering was sharp on the enclosed air.

"Let yourself off the hook, MacAlindon. Tell us what we want to know."

After the first hour or so he had been ordered to inch his feet away from the wall—two inches, maybe three. Every thirty minutes he was forced to repeat the move, increasing the pressure on his thumbs and fingers. Now he was straining at a forty-five-degree angle and a gale was roaring inside his head.

"We can wait, of course," the corporal said, parade-

40

ground style. "The whole day long if need be. Another fucking night on top if that's what you want." A match flared and he lit a cigarette. "But you'll tell us in the end—they all do. So why not save yourself the trouble?"

The man groaned again and tried to lift his head.

Some Judas had given him away. To begin with he had thrashed coldly around inside himself for a likely suspect, a possible reason why, but his mind had long since gone beyond conscious usefulness. His spine felt as if it was about to snap in two and his legs were beginning to shake uncontrollably.

"Let's recap, shall we?" A chair scraped on the floor, and the major stood up. He had a quieter voice and a different style, but nothing else was any different. "Let's remind ourselves why we're here, shall we?"

No answer.

"Shall we, MacAlindon?"

He spaced it out, and it all took time, excruciating time. The man screwed his eyes and tried to hide away inside his own throbbing blood-red darkness. Six hours and he was losing control of himself. Six hours and he was about to crack, the pain that was screaming through every part of him threatening to betray the remnants of his resolve.

"You came out the back of number fourteen Kilbrennan Street just as entry was made at the front. . . . Remember that?"

The major waited, then gave a small shrug.

"There was no one in the house except you. And nothing much in the house except what was under the floor downstairs."

Again there was no answer, but the major remained unperturbed. He knew what he was doing. The old-fashioned pressures were still the best.

"Your name's not in dispute. Driving license, rent book, medical certificate—hell, you might as well have been wearing an identity disc. MacAlindon . . . Sean MacAlindon,

41

electrician, self-employed . . . But what about the stuff under the floor? What about *that*? That's really something out of the ordinary, wouldn't you say?"

Silence. The major measured his man, one card left to play and holding it back, biding his time. He watched beads of sweat splash darkly on the floor and saw how the heavy body shuddered.

Soon now, he told himself.

"Up on your toes, MacAlindon," the corporal prodded. "Up, up . . . *Up!*"

Cigarette smoke stung the major's eyes. Six hours of this and not an iota given away; in any other circumstances he might have marveled.

"Tell me something."

So patient, so calculated.

"Under the floor in the house you rent we found a control handset and a supply of special detonators." For the nth time. "Would that be a Touchbutton by any chance?"

The man moaned and gasped. Nothing more.

"Who supplied you?"

Nothing more, but near the end of his tether.

"Did you go south, or was it delivered?"

Nothing.

The major shot the corporal a sharp glance. "Who supplied you, MacAlindon? Tell me that and you can come off the wall."

He watched the climax of the man's agony for a final few seconds. Then, head cocked, he played his card.

"What would you say if I told you it was . . . Brendan Nolan?"

The man went down as though he'd taken a karate chop, straight down like a dead man, and the major pistoned his hands triumphantly together, one into the other.

"Hold out most of the night," he said to the corporal. "And then—bingo!—suddenly it's all been in vain."

A thin pale smile of satisfaction crinkled his face as he

looked at the body heaped unconscious on the floor. There were times when it paid to gamble.

"Mention of Nolan took him right between the eyes."

"What time is it?"

"Seven," Anna Dabrowska told Leach. *"Siedem . . ."*

"Lessons in bed?"

"Where else?" Curled lips and waiting eyes, first thing in the morning. "Where better?"

He reached for her and pulled her close. She was smooth and warm and laughing.

"I was lucky to find you," he said. "Chance really took me by the arm that day. We're two of a kind."

"Dziekuje bardzo . . . Thank you very much."

"You shouldn't be so patronizing. It could do you no end of harm."

"I'll have them put that on my gravestone."

He made love to her then, swiftly and fiercely, and when their wildness was at its peak she cried out in ecstasy. Later, spent and separated, with their bodies strewn untidily across the bed, Leach stared at her with total contentment.

"What was it you said?"

"When?"

"You screamed a bit. Right into my ear."

"Oh." She smiled. "Oh, that couldn't be translated."

"Couldn't be or won't be?"

"Couldn't."

He tutted. "And you a scholar, too."

It was strange, but there were days when he could hardly believe there had been a time when she didn't exist for him, a time when she hadn't laid claim to his mind and his body. November now, only November, four months at most since their meeting in the Old Town, yet already—in thought and deed—she was indispensable to him. The sum total of eighteen days together and it had come to this.

"About last night," he began.

"Yes?"

"I've been thinking."

Anna frowned slightly. "Is this a new game? If so, I would like to know how to play."

"You said something about leaving here. About coming with me."

She held back for a second or two, as if the thought now alarmed her. "Leaving Poland, you mean?"

"Of course."

"It is impossible."

"Why?"

"I told you. I told you before."

"Because of your sister?"

"Correct."

"I can't believe you're permanently restricted because of that. I'm not doubting your word, but it does seem to me—"

"Go and ask them, Martin. I had an opportunity to go abroad only last year—to Paris. But I could not. I was not allowed."

"How long would you've been in Paris?"

"Two weeks only."

"And they said no?"

"Uh-huh."

"How long is it since your sister went to the States?"

"Six years."

Leach whistled softly. "That's bloody." If she had told him this as well, it had escaped his mind. He slid a hand over the trough of her wrist. "Just because one person in a family gets a black mark against her name—"

"There is another reason, Martin."

"What's that?"

"My work."

"Printing?"

She nodded. "Government printing."

A boat hooted on the river, the sound low and mournful. The world was out there, waiting for them.

"So?" Leach said.

"Military printing."

"I didn't know that." He was surprised. "Secret, you mean? Classified?"

"Yes." She seemed almost nervous for a moment. "What we print is technical, for specialists. It is to do with weapons and armaments. The circulation is limited."

"I see." Then he said: "Don't you work there as a secretary?"

"Secretary and assistant."

"Assistant?"

"To the head of a department."

"Ah."

"It . . . it is better if we do not talk about this any more." Uneasiness was still there, just below the surface. "Do you understand?"

"Okay."

All at once her anxiety that he shouldn't come to her office made better sense. And her choosing out-of-town restaurants. *And* their walking in the summer evening dusk where the crowds did not go.

"Okay," he said. "I reckon I've got the picture now."

"My work, and my sister. The two things combined. That is why there are such difficulties for me."

"Yes," he said thoughtfully. "Yes."

A small fraction of the day went by, their eyes meeting, Leach gently fingering the line where Anna's hair grew away from her forehead.

"I should have explained this to you earlier."

"It doesn't matter."

"It does," she said. "Everything about us matters. But I wasn't sure how much I should tell you."

"Don't look so serious."

A smile flickered and he tried to encourage it.

"Secrecy corrupts. And absolute secrecy corrupts absolutely—didn't you know?"

"I don't like the sound of that at all."

"I love you."

"I like that better," she said. "Much, much better."

"It also happens to be true."

She touched him, whole worlds of meaning in the gesture. "It's not just this, then?"

"No, it's not just this." With others, yes; but not with her. "Surely you know by now."

Later, in the tiny alcove next to her kitchen, with a window looking out on the broad river and the traffic heading downtown over the Poniatowski bridge, they drank black coffee and he smoked cigarettes. In twenty minutes she would leave for the office. Not long afterwards he would let himself out and make his way to where he garaged the Saxon mobile unit. Towards evening they would meet again and rediscover each other, then sleep and awake to another dawn and another separation. And in four days' time they would cling together in good-bye and he would head the unit west to Leipzig and on to Rotterdam.

Anna must have read his mind. "How long can we survive? . . . I ask you."

She was like a child sometimes, so direct. She shook her head almost ruefully and frowned at Leach across the table.

"Like this, how long?"

He felt a slight contraction in his gut, like a fist clenching.

"I love you, too," she went on. "And for me that means

making a life together, really together. Openly. Not this way, not with me like some whore you come to visit when you have the chance. . . . This is no good, Martin."

He was ahead of her. A hundred times faster than speech he telescoped the possibilities, weighing what would be put in jeopardy.

"If you were to come with me—"

He broke off, thinking of Warrick and the agreement entered into and the money so far earned—one thousand pounds for every delivery, one thousand clear in a numbered Swiss account. So much was already at risk, not merely his future with Saxon Engineering; he was in deep as it was. "You're greedy," Warrick had said, but to hell with that. He knew what he was doing and what it was worth. And so did Warrick's lords and masters; they'd paid all right, good as gold, on the nail.

"We've got to be sure, Anna. Absolutely cast-iron sure. Both of us."

"I am." She was grave and intense, her gaze never leaving him. "I have never in my life been so sure."

"About me?"

"Of course about you."

"Only me?" He gripped her hands. "It's not because I'm a means to an end?"

"No."

"You could delude yourself, you see—"

"No!" she flashed.

"Forgive me, but you must ask yourself these things. You have to, in fairness to us both. Because once we commit ourselves there'll be no going back."

"I know that."

"There's only one way I can think of getting you out, and that's by smuggling you through in the unit."

He listened to what he was saying as if someone else were talking. Four months ago it would have sounded like

47

madness. But at last a woman had found a crack in his heart and entered him there, changing him, making him a stranger to himself.

"When, Martin?"

Again he felt the pressure in the pit of his stomach, a kind of fear, and in the same fraction of a second he was aware that the choice had already been made; and it seemed to him then that from the very beginning, by the Ruch shop, from her opening "Can I help you, please?" the decision had somehow been inevitable and ordained, like the turning of the earth.

"When?" Excitement shone in the trembling green eyes.

"Next month?" He looked away. "Before then would be impossible."

They were talking about December, late December. And it was still madness. There were short-term risks and possible long-term repercussions, any one of which could bring disaster landsliding down. On the day of his death-in-the-heart handshake with Warrick at Galatorsko a part of him accepted that he could never be comfortable any more, never quite safe. But that was before he fell in love, and love seemed suddenly like a shield.

"I've got business obligations, Anna. What I do, and when I can do it, depends a lot on others."

He thought of Retman then, Marek Retman, Retman who was Warrick's go-between. Retman would have to be told that nothing would be carried in December. For one month, one month only, there would be no load packed into the space behind the display cabinets. For one month only Brendan Nolan would have to go without.

Anna drained her cup. "How would you manage it?"

He hesitated, pushing back his chair. "I'm not sure." Some things she must never know. "It'll take some working out."

"Would it be difficult?"

"Easier for me than for most, I'd say."

"Dangerous?"

"To a point." He smiled at her. "Don't worry so . . . And don't rush your fences. We don't have to decide everything in the next five minutes."

She rose from the table and hurried to him, flinging her arms around his neck. "Martin . . . Martin." Time and again she kissed him, murmuring, laughing a little, and he held her close in an intensity of feeling. When she drew away he saw that her eyes were huge with tears and her lips were trembling.

"What do I say?"

In all his life Leach had never known such a look. He cupped her face impulsively in his hands. Lies had become his stock in trade and he was swept by a craving for truth and its simplicity.

"Say you love me."

"I do, I do."

"That's it. That's everything."

Out on the river a boat's siren hooted again. Over and over he was to remember the sound of it and the tearstains of joy on Anna's cheeks and the startled way she suddenly said, "My God, the time," and began hurrying into her coat and knee-length boots, laughing then, both of them laughing with a kind of relief.

"Where would we cross the frontier?"

"Leknics. They know me well enough there. I'm pretty much a regular, back and forth."

"And then?" Anna glanced hurriedly at herself in a mirror. "Where then?"

"Leipzig . . . Leipzig, Magdeburg, Hanover, Rotterdam —that kind of thing."

"I can't believe it, Martin." She shook her head, amazement in her expression. "An hour ago and this was just another day."

"For me as well."

She had gone to the front door. Now she paused there

with a hand on the latch. All at once they had become conspirators.

"It's true, isn't it? It's not a dream?"

"Idiot."

"You won't have changed your mind by this evening?"

"Why do you say that?"

"It . . . it is such an enormous thing." She came back a little way, uncertain and almost afraid. What a language the face can speak. "Not just the going, I mean. Afterwards, the problems, afterwards, for you as well as me. We haven't even begun to talk about what's involved."

"We'll talk tonight," he said. "We'll talk and talk and talk."

"Tonight's too far away. Could you meet me at one o'clock?"

"Of course."

"And you won't change your mind?"

He never forgot that desperate need for reassurance: it moved him terribly.

"I won't change my mind," he told her. "Ever."

📶 10

"Right," the Home Secretary said. He wore a small neat beard around a small untidy mouth and he said "Right" at every conceivable opportunity, as if to impress on Howard that he was taking everything in. "Well, with any luck Chisholm's going to confirm that we've at least got our hands on a Touchbutton." He glanced up from the pad on which he doodled incessantly. "Is having one likely to be of any help to you?"

"Only if it's stamped with the maker's name and address."

"I thought, perhaps, that it might be possible to make certain deductions—technical deductions," he interpolated vaguely, "based on what Chisholm finds."

"As to source, you mean?"

"Right."

"I don't know about deductions," Howard said. "We might be able to make a guess, I suppose. But then, we're pretty used to that. We've been guessing for weeks."

They were alone. It was barely nine-fifteen, yet Howard was the third appointment in the morning's diary.

"According to my information," the Home Secretary said, "there's every reason now to link Touchbutton with the Provisionals' splinter group C.I.V.A."

He was talking about the extremist Committee for Irish Volunteer Action.

"I gather that interrogation overnight has as good as yielded Brendan Nolan's name."

" 'As good as'?"

"It's not in writing. And they retract their admissions, as you know."

Howard grunted.

"Does the news surprise you?"

"Not about C.I.V.A. I'd have thought that was longish odds on. But Nolan, Brendan Nolan—that's interesting."

"Tell me why."

"One, because he's a known C.I.V.A. quartermaster. And, two, because to the best of my knowledge he's stayed south of the border for a helluva long time."

The Home Secretary blinked as he doodled. "Meaning?"

"That if your information's correct, it would be fair to assume that Touchbutton deliveries are made to the Republic."

"And distributed from there?"

Howard nodded.

"You've always thought this possible, haven't you?"

"Probable," he stressed.

Four nights ago the Home Secretary had gone on television nationwide and spoken emotionally about the unspeakable wickedness of the new bombing onslaught, appealing for public calm and co-operation, spelling out in heavy detail the increased restrictions clamped on civil liberties and hinting cryptically at the unprecedented security measures in operation. "We are dealing with psychopaths," he declaimed. "Make no mistake about it. I urge you all to face up to the terror they are using against us with vigilance and resolution. . . ." For someone who, because of a Cabinet reshuffle, had inherited the hottest seat in the government almost simultaneously with the first Touchbutton claim, it was a gravely powerful and impressive performance. But here, in the privacy of his oak-paneled office, with its drab green curtains and a photograph of his wife staring disapprovingly at him from a large chintz-covered settee, he was far less sure of himself. Touchbutton was a murderous refinement added to a prolonged campaign of widespread and indiscriminate slaughter, and the Ministry of Health, his previous appointment, must have seemed like a cakewalk in comparison with what he'd got now.

And there was so much detail to digest, so many new names to have on the tip of one's tongue, so few hours in the day.

"What about this fellow—" he flipped his fingers— "Warrick? I read that report of yours. You see him as a key figure in all this."

"Very possibly."

"Defected, right? Went over to the Russians a year or two back?"

"That's correct."

"Recap on him for me."

"Warrick was a staff sergeant in the Royal Engineers,

based in Berlin. He's thirty-six years old—now, that is. The summer before last he was reported absent from his unit and, some weeks later, he turned up in Moscow. Since then he has two or three times been noted on the scene at various pressure points—in Beirut, for instance, in Cyprus more recently, and once—only last week—in Algiers. All the indications are that he's been put to work in the terrorist field. Not actively, more as a controller and general coordinator."

"Recruitment?"

"That, too."

"Is there anything to suggest he's in any way linked with groups operating within the U.K.?"

"Not specifically," Howard answered. "But that doesn't mean—"

"You keep tabs on him, though?"

"In as far as it's possible to keep tabs on him. Warrick's something of a will-o'-the-wisp. The ones I *do* keep tabs on are a lot nearer home."

The Home Secretary looked at his watch and frowned. Howard increased his pace; there was never enough time.

"As late as yesterday I was especially interested in a short list of eighteen—though that's now been reduced by one."

"Eighteen suspects?"

"Not exactly. The police can deal with the out-and-out suspects. We're casting an altogether wider net. I'm in need of three answers about Touchbutton—where they come from, how they're supplied, who delivers. Most of the people on the short list put themselves there by the very nature of their background and their travels and contacts abroad. Other special factors occasionally need taking into consideration, but those are the principal combinations."

"How do they get *off* this short list of yours?"

"Mostly they expose themselves. There's usually no smoke without fire."

"Explain that."

53

"Yesterday, for example," Howard said, "G Section advised that surveillance of a particular steward on a British coaster making the Rostock–Gravesend run wasn't worth the candle any more." He sketched a small jerky gesture to end on. "Cameras and watches—that's someone else's baby."

"So you're left with seventeen?"

"At present. And it's blindman's buff."

The Home Secretary glanced up sharply from his endless doodling. At ten o'clock he was due to receive a deputation of provincial civic leaders, who would press yet again for the return of capital punishment. The media were beginning to clamor for it, and public opinion was hardening. Touch-button could well turn out to be the final straw.

"Of these seventeen," he began, then paused in mid-sentence as it struck him suddenly how worn Howard looked; the twitching mouth, the veins like cords beside the eyes. "Of these seventeen," he repeated, "do any of your investigations show more promise than others?"

"One."

"Tell me."

Howard removed a brown Manila file from his briefcase and opened it up on the big desk. From the file he extracted a black-and-white photograph, which he passed across to the Home Secretary.

"Taken last June," he explained, "at a place called Galatorsko, in Poland. Don't concern yourself with those lying at the side of the pool or the person on the diving board. Concentrate on the two on the left, the two who're standing together."

"What about them?"

"The one facing the camera is Warrick."

"And the other?"

Close by in Whitehall a car backfired and they flinched, both of them, nerves and imagination allied. Neither took refuge in a subsequent shamefaced smile or gesture. This was how the real thing happened—no warning, no time to steel oneself; they were living with it.

"And the other?" Howard was asked again.

"His name's Leach . . . Martin Graham Leach."

"Go on."

Howard checked with the file. "I'd better say straight away that he's clean. In the U.K. he's clean. . . . I'll come to that in a minute."

"Right."

"Leach is employed by Saxon Engineering. Saxon is London based, and he works for it as an overseas rep. Poland, Czechoslovakia, and East Germany, once in a while in Hungary—they're his principal stamping grounds. This side of the Soviet bloc he takes in Holland and West Germany, though only after a fashion, mainly in passing."

"Some territory."

"He's a commercial tourist who operates a traveling showcase for Saxon—films, literature, sample exhibits. . . . You know the kind of thing. . . . Although he's London based himself, he spends anywhere up to three weeks in every month out of the country. But he comes and goes. By its very nature a job like that gives him unrivaled opportunities for being a carrier, or a linkman or whatever."

"When did you get hold of this picture?"

"Midsummer."

Howard toyed with adding that Petrie was responsible, then decided against it: one more name might only confuse.

"What's the name of the place you mentioned?"

"Galatorsko. It's a holiday center about a couple of hundred miles south of Warsaw. There's a residential press club near the village. You're looking at the club's pool and surroundings."

The Home Secretary peered closely at the photograph. "Tell me some more about Leach."

"Unmarried, no brothers and sisters, widowed mother

lives at Bromley. He himself has a flat in west London at Brook Green. Criminal Records has checked out his known contacts and they seem innocuous enough. No significant Irish connections and not all that many friends—of any description. He's something of a loner. Special Branch has searched his flat, and we've tapped his phone during his last two visits home, but nothing's come of it."

Howard frowned. So much of this sounded like a classic dead end.

"He's clean, as I said. Yet, even so," he insisted, "he's the one where I'm most inclined to hang my hat."

"Because of the photograph?"

"Mainly because of the photograph."

"It could have been chance, couldn't it, the two of them being at the place together?"

"Long odds against, I'd say."

"But it could have been?"

"Possibly."

"So?" The Home Secretary shifted irritably. Don't waste my time, his tone implied.

"Warrick's no fool. He wouldn't have let the opportunity go by—even if their meeting *was* coincidental. Not with his track record. Someone like Leach would have been manna from heaven."

"Always assuming Warrick is actually cast in the role you see for him." Rain tapped softly at the window. "And then only if Leach was prepared to make himself useful."

"Pressures can be brought to bear."

"Blackmail?"

"Or inducements."

"Hmmmm." The Home Secretary fingered the surface of the desk like someone reading Braille. "It seems to me you're on dreadfully thin ice."

"True."

"I must confess I'd rather hoped you would have more for me than this."

Stung, Howard said: "We aren't merely looking for a needle in a haystack. It isn't that easy. As things stand we aren't even sure which haystack to choose."

They heard the rain again; it must have just started.

"You could have him picked up."

Howard shook his head.

"Pump him dry. "

"I don't want that."

"Under the new powers he could be held for long enough to—"

"I don't want that. Not yet, anyway. I want to see where he leads us."

"And if it's nowhere?"

Howard said heavily: "Then I'll have a lot to answer for."

"Time isn't on our side."

"I know." Jesus.

"We can't afford to allow the initiative—"

"I *know*." Howard didn't want to listen to the obvious. "But I'm ready to bet there's more to Leach than meets the eye, and in my considered opinion it's important to see if we can use him. Pick him up and God knows what we might lose long-term."

The Home Secretary pursed his lips. He didn't like these open-ended situations, least of all when he was ultimately answerable. Results were what he needed most, some kind of victory, something to tell his Cabinet colleagues and the House of Commons.

"You seem so sure about him," he conceded.

"Far from it. But certain facts single him out."

"More than any of the others you mentioned?"

"His credentials, if that's the word, are more significant."

"Being photographed with Warrick?"

"That's not quite all," Howard said. "Leach and Warrick were noted at Galatorsko in midsummer, on the twenty-seventh of June, to be exact. The twenty-seventh of June

57

is when the picture was taken. Within a month of that date we'd checked Leach's background inside out and slapped a tail on him while he was in this country." He paused. "I think perhaps I ought to give you the kind of schedule he normally keeps."

"Right."

"After about a week or so back in Saxon's head office he flies out to Rotterdam, where the firm's exhibition trailer is garaged throughout his absence in London. From there he travels east to undertake his assignments, and approximately three weeks later—give or take a few days—he returns to Rotterdam and then flies to Heathrow. Inquiries have shown this has been his regular work pattern over the last eighteen or twenty months."

"And now it's changed?"

"Not exactly. But it changed once. It changed in August."

"In what way?"

"Leach was missing for a week." Howard held up a hand to ward off further interruptions. "We haven't so far had the co-operation we might have expected this side of the Communist bloc. It's difficult to get precisely the right weight of support when you're at the start of a waiting game, and we've everywhere stressed the necessity of keeping as low a profile as possible. But there's no doubt he was missing after getting to Rotterdam three months ago."

"When homeward bound?"

Howard nodded. "He normally flies over within hours of arriving, but in August he didn't. The trailer was garaged as usual, but six whole days went by before Leach turned up at Heathrow."

The Home Secretary stopped his doodling. He was a politician to his fingertips, which meant he survived by picking other people's brains.

"What particular significance do you attach to that?"

"I think we should bear two things in mind. One, that

the first Touchbutton claim was made in September—just eleven weeks after Leach and Warrick met at Galatorsko. And, two, that it happened the month after Leach ducked from sight at Rotterdam."

"You're saying—?"

"I'm saying that during the week in question he could have made the run to Ireland and back. . . . *Could* have, mind you."

"By boat?"

"Fast power boat. Either coast to coast or to an offshore rendezvous."

"In August?"

"I'm suggesting that, yes." No imagination, Howard thought accusingly. No bloody imagination at all. "It could easily have been done. There was time enough."

"Why not since?"

"I can't even pretend to know." At the back of his mind he was aware of the rain like tears on the windows and a pewter-dull sky beyond. "Perhaps he made the first run to establish personal contact. Perhaps there hasn't been another since. Perhaps, if a delivery *was* made in September, he left the seagoing to someone else." He fluttered his hands and snorted, months of exasperation and nothing to show. "Perhaps it isn't he at all."

"Hmmm," the Home Secretary said. There was silence for what seemed a long time—fifteen or twenty seconds, maybe. Then, as if he had reached a decision with himself, he looked at his watch again and said: "And you would still prefer not to have him questioned?"

"Not yet."

"I must say it sounds as if you've got your hooks into something more than I supposed."

"Only perhaps." Nerves plucked at the side of Howard's mouth. "The day I can pin him down to some specific connection with this business—that'll be the day."

"Where is he now?"

"Warsaw."

"Due home?"

"A week from now."

"We could have the Dutch put his trailer under the microscope at the frontier."

"That would be the end of him as far as we're concerned—whether he was running a delivery or not. Warrick and Company would drop him like a hot potato."

"If you suspect him, you'll have to move eventually."

"I want more than the delivery boy. Take this one out and they'll find others. We'll be back where we began."

"Very well." The Home Secretary started gently massaging the surface of his desk again. "I'm sure you know what you're doing"—and somehow he made it sound almost like a threat.

Howard rose to his feet; he'd been there longer than he'd ever thought possible.

"Say Leach *is* involved," the Home Secretary remarked as he accompanied Howard across the room. "What do you suppose could have persuaded him?"

"When he met Warrick, d'you mean?"

"That's it. After all, your inquiries seem to indicate there's nothing in his past to link him with terrorism."

"Which made him ideal material."

"But what would Warrick have used to make him go to work?"

"I'm only guessing," Howard pointed out.

"Right."

"Greed?" He let it hang there. "Greed's usually the cause of lift-off for amateurs—and Leach sounds like one of those to me."

"If it's he."

"Quite. There's always that."

They shook hands.

"Keep in daily touch," the Home Secretary insisted and

said good-bye. With those untidy teeth of his he never smiled, even at the best of times.

Outside, on the corner, the placard headlines read: ANOTHER TOUCHBUTTON?

Howard noted them with eyes narrowed against the rain. But for the rain, he would have walked to Buckingham Gate, but as it was he took a taxi—five minutes from door to door, only Great George Street and Birdcage Walk in between, Wellington Barracks soon flicking past behind the railings on his left and the Palace almost directly ahead.

If anywhere was Touchbutton territory, surely this was it.

"Morning, Mr. Howard."

"Morning."

He rode up to the third in a crowded lift. Jenny Knight was still off sick, and Sheard had gone to Belfast with Chisholm; he'd all but forgotten that until he saw the unfamiliar way the stuff awaiting attention was stacked on his desk.

For a while it could wait, though. He rang Vaughan in the general office.

"What's this about another Touchbutton?"

"There's been an incident at Hampton Court. A bus blown up."

"Tourists?"

"Royal Marine bandsmen."

"Oh, Christ."

"First reports are pretty bad."

"Has a claim been made?"

"Not yet. But it wouldn't surprise me. This one's got Touchbutton stamped all over it."

"Thanks," Howard said and hung up, surprised the Home Secretary hadn't been notified while they were together. Perhaps he didn't tolerate interruptions unless they concerned successes—in which case, he must have had precious few recently: none, even.

61

The telephone buzzed. "Howard." It was Vaughan again.

"I forgot to mention that your son called. He wondered if you'd lunch with him."

"Today?"

"One o'clock at the Open Arms. He said to tell you that if you can't make it he'll quite understand."

"Did he leave a number?"

"No."

Typical, Howard thought. "Very well."

Frowning, he sat down and reached for the first of the day's files, his mind at the center of a multiple tug-of-war between imagined scenes at Hampton Court and how Chisholm and Sheard were making out in Belfast and the morning's account to the Home Secretary of Leach's known activities. . . .

And Colin, suddenly Colin.

Colin rang.

All at once he remembered Eve's note propped against the alarm clock at home, and for a long and lonely moment he could think only of Eve and his own bitter failure towards dawn.

 **11**

Philip Chisholm reckoned the Touchbutton handset weighed about three pounds.

It was a fraction larger than he'd supposed from the overnight telephone description—nine inches by six, to be precise, and four inches deep. The heavy-gauge black plastic casing was in two sections, base and cover plates secured by white metal screws at each corner. Set in circular recesses in the cover plate were two dumpy red buttons. The base plate was grooved to facilitate a person's grip, and when held in both hands the thumbs settled comfortably over the buttons.

Chisholm grunted. A small lever like one half of a wing nut protruded from the left side of the casing. "What d'you think? Safety catch?"

"I'd say so." The brigadier nodded. "Some kind of locking pin, probably."

There were no markings on the casing, no markings on the lead-lined canister that held the detonators, no markings on the stout wooden box that housed both the canister and the handset.

Chisholm turned the handset upside down. The over-all finish was poor. "Nobody's looked inside?" He'd insisted on inaction, not even a partial turn of the screws, but he wanted it confirmed.

"No, sir," the brigadier said. "Nothing's been tampered with. We've had a detonator out of the canister, but that's all."

He took one out now and handed it carefully across. It was cylindrical, about three inches long and half an inch in diameter; the sheathing was aluminum bright with a thin purple stripe smudged along its length.

"Big," Chisholm commented.

They were in an old Nissen hut on the army's small-arms range northeast of Belfast—Chisholm and the brigadier and Sheard, a major and a warrant officer from R.E.M.E. and an Ordnance Corps captain of the bomb-disposal squad. No range master, no control party, nobody but themselves. A staff car had been waiting at the airport for Chisholm and Sheard, bringing them straight here, and it was a measure of the importance of what they'd come to see that the brigadier was there to greet them.

"What we've laid on," the brigadier said crisply, "is an opportunity for you to experiment with the thing."

"Up to what range?"

"Two thousand yards. We've got markers in position at one hundred, five hundred, one and two thousand."

"Show me, would you?"

"Right away."

They went outside. The air was raw; after the fog of the Nissen hut it watered their eyes. The hut stood only a stone's throw from the firing butts, and the various ranges pointed into the distance like the fingers of a splayed hand, four of them, the earthworks behind each target area humped brown against the grey-green horizon. On the thousand-yard range a flock of seagulls patched the scarred ground like snow.

"I won't bother with the five hundred," Chisholm said.

"Very well."

"Six detonators isn't much to play with, and I'll want to take a couple back with me. The effect of screening interests me as much as anything."

The squad bomb-disposal captain said: "The canister lining's obviously proof against simultaneous detonation."

"I was thinking of signal deflection generally. To begin with, though—" Chisholm gave the brigadier a craggy glance—"d'you think you could rig something up along the lines of a charge encased in a milk churn?"

"Shouldn't be difficult. See what you can do, Roberts."

The warrant officer put his notebook away and moved off purposefully to one of the waiting jeeps.

"A galvanized bucket'll suit," Chisholm called after him. "That kind of thing—okay?"

"Where d'you want to start?" the brigadier asked. "At a hundred yards?"

Chisholm nodded.

"Screened or unscreened?"

"Unscreened. First and foremost I want to check that

the thing does what we expect it to. No more than that right now."

"Why two buttons?" the major asked, wiping a pinched red nose.

"Probably because the detonator incorporates a double coil and nothing is activated unless both buttons are depressed. We'll find out soon enough, but that's my guess. There has to be a safeguard against accidental detonation by anyone operating on the same frequency—radio hams or the police, for instance."

"Do you suppose," Sheard said thoughtfully, "that each Touchbutton operates on a different frequency?"

"Each handset and its complement of half-a-dozen detonators, d'you mean?"

"Exactly."

"Until we get hold of another one we'll never know."

"Otherwise," Sheard persisted, "with two or three operators in the same area, God knows what cross firing could result."

"You've got a point there," the brigadier agreed and stared down at his feet as though he'd never seen them before. "Yes, quite a point."

The captain went back to the hut for the wooden box. The handset he passed to Chisholm. One of the detonators he then extracted from its canister and rode with it in the remaining jeep to the hundred-yard target area.

"Lead-lined or not, I don't exactly trust that damned container," Chisholm muttered. "Not this close, anyway."

The brigadier took it over to the sand pit by the firing butt and buried it there, scooping out a hole with his hands and then heeling the sand firm. He was all arms and legs, with an extraordinarily long neck. Action suited him: his lean, totem-pole face didn't look so blank while he was doing something. As soon as he returned he called the target area on the spotter's field telephone.

"How're you fixed?" A small cold breeze whipped them

suddenly. "All set? . . . Good." He listened for a while before saying "Take cover, then."

"Ready?" Chisholm asked.

"Ten seconds, sir," the brigadier cautioned, and raised his binoculars. "The detonator's directly in front of target number four. It's been placed on the raised lip of the area, two sandbags off the ground."

"Right," Chisholm said.

Everyone was suddenly very still.

"I'm releasing the locking pin." Chisholm turned the small lever through one hundred and eighty degrees. "Now I'm going to depress the right-hand button."

A couple of seconds elapsed, Chisholm standing rather hunched with the handset held waist high. Then there was a slight click, and five pairs of eyes strained towards the indicated target.

"Nothing," the brigadier announced, skepticism at the ready.

"Left-hand button . . . *Now*."

Instantly they saw the flash. Almost simultaneously the seagulls on the neighboring range rose, startled, into the air. A split second later the sharp crack of the explosion reached them.

"Bingo!" Chisholm jerked out.

"Fantastic!"—Sheard.

Chisholm lifted his thumbs off the buttons.

"Everything I expected . . . *and* feared. It works, that's the hell of it." He clamped the locking pin back on. "Can we go to the other extreme now and try it out at two thousand?"

"Anything you say." The brigadier nodded. "God, that's a gadget and a half."

He cranked the field telephone and called the captain back from the target area, then dug the canister out of the sand and removed another detonator. The captain brought the jeep bumping down the track between the ranges at top speed, collected the detonator, and set off at a more cautious pace.

"No screening?" the brigadier inquired. "Same as before?"

"No screening, but let's give it some explosive to cut its teeth on."

Industry had dabbled with something along the lines of Touchbutton, Chisholm reminded himself. At the back of his mind was a hazy recollection of experiments carried out in opencast coal mining. Sometime, somewhere. He frowned at what was in his hands, grey hair ruffled, big mouth gaping slightly. He seemed quite oblivious of the cold, unaware of the others, gone into himself.

"Are you all right?" Sheard asked him.

"Of course." He grimaced. "Started a hare and then lost it."

Too hazardous for industry, he concluded. And too damned expensive, anyhow.

They watched the jeep dwindle. The seagulls were beginning to settle in another part of the range. About ten minutes after the first explosion the brigadier and the captain were again in contact, while the warrant officer had returned from heaven knows where with a couple of battered fire buckets.

"Position's as before, sir," the brigadier called. "Directly in front of the number four target."

Chisholm widened his stance and went through the selfsame drill. Everyone peered as before, but only the brigadier, glued to his binoculars, saw the small discolored flash. "Yep," he shouted. "That's it." And then the sound came in confirmation, a celery snap, blurred and distorted by the breeze.

The major whistled. "Right on."

"Every time a bull's eye," Chisholm said. "Let's try one with the detonator completely shielded."

"Same distance?"

"Come back a thousand and don't bother about taping it to a charge."

"Will do."

The captain perched the detonator on a mound of earth six inches high and covered it with one of the buckets, twisting the rim into the ground. Heath Robinson, but adequate: the clinical tests must wait for another time, another place. Presently he reported the all clear and the brigadier passed the word to Chisholm.

"Locking pin released . . . Right-hand button . . . Left-hand button . . ."

Nothing happened.

"Aaaah."

They waited about ten seconds. The breeze tugged this way and that.

"You see?" Chisholm said excitedly. "Hang on and I'll do a repeat."

Again nothing happened. Next he reversed the order of depressing the buttons; after which he rammed them down simultaneously. Neither time was there a detonation.

"Thought as much. Signal deflection. That's its drawback, all right. Metal does it, obviously." He hesitated. So much needed to be proved. "But in urban districts I'd have thought the signal stood every chance of being made ineffective for all sorts of reasons. Unless there's a direct shot, that is. Same probably applies to open country if the target's on a reverse slope, say, or generally obscured."

The brigadier said: "It can't operate around corners, you mean?"

"Exactly." Chisholm pursed his lips grimly. "What a helluva weapon, though. And how in the name of Christ do you stop 'em using it?"

He thought of Howard as he spoke, Howard on whom so much of the burden lay. "I don't know what we're looking for yet"—only last night, in Fisher's, Howard had said that;

so progress had been made. Some, anyway. At least they weren't in the dark any more.

"What next, sir?"

"I'd think I'd like to have a shot at testing the screening effectiveness of something bulky—the earth mound behind the target areas, for example." Like many big men Chisholm was never less than courteous, a fact that pleased the brigadier. Too many civilians believed they were God almighty. "Do you suppose we could return to the hundred-yard range?"

They withdrew to where they had started, not far from the solitary Nissen hut. For another forty minutes Chisholm improvised his field tests. By noon he'd exploded one more detonator and was ready to call a halt. The major's nose was scarlet by this time and Sheard's fingers had gone numb.

"What about lunch?" The brigadier wanted to know, shuffling his feet like someone about to be found short.

"Beer and a sandwich for me," Chisholm said. "Mr. Sheard and I are hoping to take an afternoon flight to London." That pleased Sheard. "But first I want to open up the handset and, if possible, get inside the detonator itself. Where can that be done?"

The major said: "I reckon you'll have to come to base workshop."

"Nearby?"

"Fifteen minutes."

"Good."

"I'd better explain—we aren't geared for anything ultra-sophisticated."

"All I want's to have a quick look-see and get something on record. The handset oughtn't to present much of a problem."

"No," it was conceded.

"Perhaps we'll have to wait until we get back to London before we tackle the detonators. One sure bet, I'd have

69

thought, is that they're fitted with a mercury-filled battery and the signals make the necessary activation by means of reed switches."

"I'd mostly agree with that," the tough-looking captain said.

"Where d'you differ?"

"I did wonder if there's any possibility of the—"

"Gentlemen," the brigadier cut in, rubbing his hands. "Don't you think, gentlemen, all that can wait until we get inside?"

12

Leach ran a demonstration film of the Saxon large-diameter pipe and its uses for the benefit of a party of eight from Warsaw's Central Ministry of Public Works. They were amiable men, though initially cautious, and it was only after Leach had put the lights back on in the trailer and passed the vodka around that their caution lifted a little.

"Excellent, Mr. Leach," their spokesman said to an odd but cheerful rhythm. "Very, very interesting. Some of us have seen the Saxon vehicle from the outside, both in Warsaw itself and elsewhere. Now we are all most grateful to have seen it on the inside and to have witnessed your film. . . . Thank you, thank you again."

Leach smiled in return and handed out the glossy technical literature. He was meeting Retman at twelve-thirty and already he was uneasy about it. He'd never asked a favor of him before; or of Warrick. In the beginning *they* were the ones who'd asked the favors, Warrick in particular. "I wonder," Warrick had begun that afternoon at

Galatorsko, "I wonder if you would spare me a few minutes. . . ."

No reason to be on edge. Weren't they partners? Business partners? In which case, favors cut both ways.

"Good-bye," Leach said as the last of his audience stepped from the trailer into a day lit by a pale-yellow sun. "*Do widzenia . . . Do widzenia . . .* Remember the name of Saxon Engineering . . . *Powodzenia.*"

All that.

He shut himself in and stacked the chairs in the recess shaped to receive them, making them secure. The projector folded away, the screen rolled up, the blinds clattered aside. The unit's interior was a masterpiece of space-saving design, not a cubic centimeter wasted. The narrow spaces below and behind the two glass-fronted display cabinets weren't exceptions; stocks of catalogues and alternative trade samples normally filled both.

"What size load could you manage?" Warrick had asked him.

"Fifty or sixty kilos."

"No more?"

"I don't see how."

"What is the problem? Space limitation?"

"That, and the weight itself. The vehicle is checked on the scales three times. At three frontiers. In over a year its weight hasn't varied."

"So how would you manage the amount you've suggested?"

"Jettison an equal weight of stock for the westward run."

"Sixty kilos means around fifty of our boxes."

"If you say so," Leach agreed.

In the event, Retman and he had settled on exactly that number—twenty-five at the rear of each of the display cabinets, locked away, weight for weight the same as given on the manifest, the boxes wedged behind a false partition, which was concealed by a double layer of legitimate hardware. The sliding doors had only once been opened, and then for the most cursory of glances.

"And this is?"

At the Dutch frontier, Leach's heart in his mouth. "Reserve stock. It's all listed."

"Thank you, sir."

One thousand pounds a trip. For that kind of money he'd been ready to blind himself to the reasons why.

Leach sank down onto his haunches now and examined the space available behind one of the cabinets, measuring what room there was. It was going to be uncomfortably tight, but Anna could just about be shoehorned in. There would be air enough for short periods, and he reckoned it would be necessary for her to be walled up for only an hour or so's journey either side of each frontier.

"You won't have changed your mind by this evening?" He pictured Anna as her words re-echoed, moved and strengthened by her need for him. It was a marvelous thing to be wanted. Incredible, worth all the risks in the world. Nothing like it had ever happened to him before.

He locked up the trailer and drove it back to the garage he rented. From there to the Chopin monument in Lazienki Park, where he'd arranged to meet Retman, was all of a fifteen-minute walk, and he hurried, hatless, hands in the pockets of his heavy coat.

No delivery in December. That's all he was going to ask. Just the one month without a load . . .

He entered the park through the gate near the Botanical Gardens and turned right towards the monument, working clockwise: it was their usual rendezvous. People were everywhere walking briskly, their breath trailing like thin grey scarves. Once in a while, during the lonely times before Anna, Leach had come here on a hot Sunday at midday and listened to a piano recital, lying on the dappled grass under a tree. The trees were all bare now, stripped clean, and he was tense and on the lookout in case Retman had got there first.

"Good afternoon."

Behind him. He swung around, a squirm in his stomach as he turned. It was the voice that did it, soft, almost feminine, everything Retman was not.

"Did I keep you waiting?"

"You did." Retman laughed. "But I was early, so I do not complain."

He indicated that they should walk on. They fell into step, shoulder to shoulder, Retman half a head shorter. This was only the sixth time they had met, and they spoke German, the only language they shared.

"You are well?" Retman asked, Retman who had come to the trailer alone one August morning and introduced himself: "I am from Warrick."

"Thank you," Leach said now.

"No troubles?"

"Not exactly."

"But you wanted to see me?"

"I have a request to make."

"Yes?"

Leach delayed. They walked a few paces, nothing special to single them out: all over Warsaw men sat on benches or walked together in the parks.

"Yes?" Retman said again.

"It concerns next month. I . . . I won't be able to take a load."

"I see." No change of tone. They went another half-dozen yards in silence. "For what reason, may I ask?"

"Saxon wants me to ferry out some obsolescent stock." The lie came pat, prepared in advance. And for a moment or two it seemed that nothing more would be needed.

"In late December?"

"Yes."

"How does that affect your arrangement with us?"

"There won't be room in the unit," Leach said.

"There has to be room."

"There won't be."

"There has to be room," Retman repeated affably. He smiled sidelong at Leach, never more discomfiting then when he smiled. "I see no special problem."

"Listen," Leach said. "I'm only talking about December."

"I understand."

"This month will be normal. January, February, March, et cetera—they'll all be normal. But December's an impossibility. I'm not always my own master in these matters."

"So you have said already."

There was silence between them. Without slowing, Retman shook out a cigarette from a crumpled pack and lit it, hands cupped like a harmonica player's. He didn't offer one to Leach.

"How long have you known this?" he asked.

"Since yesterday. London sent me a Telex."

"May I see it, please?"

"I . . . I didn't keep it." The back of Leach's neck prickled. He licked his lips, partially turning his head. In profile were the astrakhan cap, the short nose, the sagging double chin. And one red-rimmed eye. "Listen," he said again. "I'm not backing down. I undertook to make ten runs, and that's what I'll do."

"Consecutive runs."

"That was never stipulated."

"August to May, inclusive."

"To the best of my ability, yes. Provided it was possible, yes. Hell, say I was taken sick in London. Say I was ill at any time and it screwed up my schedule—what then? How would—"

"*Are* you sick?"

Leach clenched his teeth. "You know damned well what I'm saying. Saxon provides the vehicle and with it the op-

portunity. They also happen to employ me. Which means
—this once, just this once—they have to be given priority."

"Does Saxon pay you a thousand a month?"

Leach didn't answer.

"In a Swiss bank? No questions asked?"

Three or four paces, as close as friends together.

"Do they?" Retman insisted. "When you talk of priorities you should ask yourself these things."

They were crossing a small stone bridge, their voices low,
neither speaking when anyone was within earshot. The
water in the channel to either side was spiked with reeds;
Leach noticed this, awareness heightened.

"This is a crucial time for supplies," Retman said. "The
build-up must continue without interruption. You will
have to make some excuse to your people, that is all there
is to it."

Leach took his time. "And if I said I can't do that?"

"Warrick would be informed."

"And—?"

"I am not in his shoes, so I cannot say." Retman picked
a strand from his thick lower lip. His soft laugh was like a
faulty lavatory flush, and a chill struck at Leach's heart.
"You see how demanding it is, this contract you have
entered into."

"Haven't I delivered? Once in person, all the way. Twice
since to Rotterdam." A couple passed, man and woman,
walking a nondescript black dog, and Leach waited until
they were clear. "This month I'll deliver again. Well, then
. . . All I'm saying—not unreasonably—is that I have to be
given an opportunity to shift this stuff for Saxon. They'll
never wait until next June. There's no possible reason for
my not complying with their instructions. When they say
December they mean December."

Retman drew a folded newspaper from an inner pocket
of his long dark coat and passed it to Leach. "Have you
read this at all?"

The *Herald Tribune.* "Not recently."

"There is a full account of the campaign's initial successes. It is essential now to ensure that the momentum is maintained."

"I don't concern myself with other people's campaigns."

"You are deaf and blind, I suppose?"

"I . . . I do what I undertook to do."

Warrick had spoken of boxes, consignments of boxes, never anything else. Not of what came after.

"What does concern you?" Retman's gaze was contemptuous. "The money, is it?"

"Why not the money?"

They were wordless for all of a hundred yards, Leach's mind prickling, a sort of nausea lying in his stomach. Through the leafless screen of trees to their left the Lazienki Palace was beginning to show, but he didn't notice. "A thousand?" he recalled Warrick saying. "Okay, it's a deal." Then came the handshake, putting a seal on the enormity of the temptation, marking the difference between whatever he used to be and whatever he had since become.

Ten thousand pounds over-all . . . The thought of it had dazzled him. Only since Anna started to grow into his life did the realization of what he was involved in begin to sicken and to scare. But he could kill it if need be; he could still kill it dead.

Retman was saying "You have no choice in this matter. It is we who have the prior claim on what you carry in December."

"I want that in writing from Warrick."

"Asking is a waste of time."

"Even so, that's what I want." Leach swallowed, pressing because of Anna, frightened because of himself. He was in deep, too deep. "On Friday I leave for Leipzig. I'll pick up a load as usual and deliver as usual. That'll be four months. Remind Warrick of that. And let me have his answer when I'm back in Warsaw again."

"I can give it to you now."

Leach stopped walking. "I do my work for Warrick."

Retman came back two paces. Middleman, contact man. But deadly dangerous.

"What else do you do, my friend? What other things?"

"What kind of question's that?"

"Professional."

"I don't understand what you mean."

"What frightens you so?" Retman stood close, close enough for Leach to see the pores in his pale coarse skin. "You are sweating, did you know?"

Leach couldn't match the searching gaze. "So?"

"That's fear, my friend." The soft laugh came. "Take care. You could drown yourself in that."

Leach came out of the park alone and stood in line at the taxi stop on Agrykola. Restless and uneasy, he waited over ten minutes for his turn.

Damn Retman.

"Grand Theatre."

The lunchtime traffic was dense and slow-moving. He fretted, his mind churning without offering any solution. Anna's weight could be coped with simply by leaving extra equipment behind—chairs, for instance; the projector and screen. No problems there. But where could Anna *and* the boxes be stowed at one and the same time? There were risks enough as it was: nerve-bending risks.

"Deep water, my friend," Retman had said as they'd separated, "is for those who can swim."

Damn Retman.

Leach paid off the taxi in the huge square in front of the Grand Theatre. He was late—five, ten minutes late—and he hated lateness. They were changing guard at the Unknown Soldier's Tomb as he arrived, the relieving three-man squad stamping its toy-soldier way across the acreage of empty paving stones. A small crowd had gathered to watch the change, and as Leach approached, he saw that Anna was already there. Tight fur hat, thick coat, knee-length boots—from a distance he recognized her without a second's hesitation. And, close to, her eyes were huge with relief at the sight of him, almost as if she secretly believed he might not come, that what they were planning was all somehow in her imagination.

"*Dzien dobry.*"

She greated him quietly in standard fashion so as not to draw attention to themselves. Leach nodded and they edged clear of the throng. The paving rang with the crash of the guards' heels. Out in the open there the sky seemed vast, streaked with streamers of cream-colored cloud.

"Well?" Anna said, linking an arm into his.

"It won't be easy."

Her expression changed. "What does that mean? Did you speak with your associates?"

"I did, yes."

"And—?"

"It's early yet, but it looks as though there are going to be difficulties."

"Oh God." Her voice was heavy with dismay. "Oh God, Martin."

"Difficulties, I said. That's all. I didn't say anything about it being impossible."

"What sort of difficulties?"

"It's more a question of timing than anything else."

Leach led her into the gardens at the rear of the colon-naded memorial. "Lies," his mother was forever saying smugly during his youth, "carry their own punishment." But he had learned to live by lies: Bromley and his youth were a long way from here and now. Warrick had come between, for one thing: Warrick, Retman, Nolan . . .

And others.

Anna, too.

She said: "Do you mean there could be a delay?"

"Delay, yes."

"Until when?"

"Next year."

"How late next year?"

"In the summer."

"Oh God," she said again. She dragged her arm away with the disappointment of a child. Then, bitterly, she said: "I might have known."

"Nothing's definite, Anna. It's just my reading of the situation. For all I know, the problems will iron themselves out."

"This morning you were so sure. So very, very sure."

Her voice trembled. He felt the weight of her distress, the pressure of it. He took her in his arms and touched her forehead with his lips.

"We'll manage," he said. "We'll make it."

She looked away. He shook her gently.

"Come *on*," he chided. "We'll make it, Anna. We'll find a way somehow. . . . You bet."

"When?"

"Just as soon as the chance is there."

"Next year . . . Sometime, never."

"No." He let go of her. "June at the latest . . . I swear to you. No later than next June."

She stayed quiet. He could read her fears. He understood them, shared them, had others all his own.

"Either next month or next June."

As if she disbelieved it all now, she said in a flat throw-away fashion: "I would have no passport anyway. If ever I did get out, I'd be heading for nothing but trouble."

"I can fix you with a passport, Anna. Someone I know can help with things like that. . . . No bother."

Her glance was swift and full of doubt.

"Really," he insisted.

79

"What kind of passport? British?"

He chose his words badly and his shrug was like a simultaneous apology. "Beggars can't be choosers."

They couldn't see, but in the square the old guard was stamping off, the staccato thud-thud-thud steadily receding.

"We'd go to England, wouldn't we?"

"Not immediately. Not you, that is."

"Where would I go then?"

He paused, scared about Retman as his thoughts raced on their way. None of this had been discussed. No details, nothing.

"I think I could get you into Ireland," he told her.

13

Howard started off by saying a bit vaguely: "You've put on weight, haven't you?"

"News to me."

"No? I'd have thought your face has filled out quite a bit."

"You don't see me often enough, that's the trouble." Colin grinned. "You're mixing me up with someone else."

"My own son?" Howard heard himself, stiff and pompous and out of touch. "What are you drinking?"

"D'you mind if I have a glass of red wine?"

"Please yourself." For some reason, he came to the Open Arms only when he met Colin. "Shall we sit at the counter, or would you prefer a table?"

"The counter'll do fine."

The place was crowded but the two end stools were that moment being vacated.

"How's Eve?" Colin asked, staking a claim to them.

"Okay."

"Still feeding good food to the cat while the world starves to death?"

"She's okay," Howard repeated carefully.

"And you?"

"Fine." His mouth twitched. "Cheers."

The Hampton Court Touchbutton bomb had been planted underneath the parked bus and detonated as the Royal Marine bandsmen climbed back in. Ten dead and others not so lucky, terribly, terribly mutilated; he had the facts now. And here he was with a glass in his hand saying "Cheers." Sometimes he felt he must be going mad.

"You've been busy, I expect," Colin said, eying him. "Up to your ears."

"Morning, noon, and night."

"This Touchbutton business—is that your pigeon?"

"In part."

"Are you getting anywhere?"

Howard drank. "Maybe."

"What's expected of you?"

"Miracles . . . What else do politicians want?"

"Can't you delegate at all?"

"Huh?"

"Don't others share the load?"

Howard said: "Do I detect the bedside manner?" He was more tart than he knew. "I was under the impression you were studying economics."

"You ought to ease up."

"Very funny."

Colin's gaze hadn't left him. "Seriously."

"Oh, for Christ's sake," Howard snapped. "Drop it, can't you?"

Above the clamor, a man nearby was building to the punch line of a joke about the Mafia, and from somewhere at the far corner of the bar there came the high shiver of a girl's laughter. Howard shifted uncomfortably, looking at the floor between his thighs. No excuses. But don't wade in so; don't crowd me.

"Sorry about that," he muttered lamely.

"I've got a right, you know."

" 'Right'?"

"To be concerned."

Howard's mouth went again. "Thanks." He nodded, moved suddenly and touched Colin on the hand. "I'm . . . I'm just a bit on edge."

"And it shows. Ten seconds and it's up in lights."

"Bad as that?"

"At least as bad as that. I'd have thought Eve would have been on at you herself."

Howard let it pass.

"Mind if I say something else?"

"Go ahead."

"You may not care for it."

"I'm getting used to not caring for things." How like Harriet he looked, Howard thought. Above the lips especially. The same good nose, the same fair lashes, the same steady eyes. Not seeing him for a while made the impression all the more striking.

"Tell me if you have to."

"You used to be more fun."

God in heaven. "Fun? . . . *Fun?*"

"That's it." Colin nodded. "Listen . . ." The girl along the bar was laughing again, no cares. "Remember?"

Howard said: "I'm not exactly in a fun situation."

"Who is these days?"

In his second year at Bristol, with everything to live for, and saying that . . . Ridiculous.

"You know, the other Sunday I was at Mass and I was only thinking—"

"You still go, then?"

"Like clockwork." Colin finished his wine. "Same again?"

"Thanks." Howard checked the time: half an hour and he must leave. He felt like a deserter here. "Could we order when you've caught someone's attention? I'll have the smoked salmon; what'll yours be?"

The top-heavy blonde behind the bar repeated everything parrot fashion, then bounced away and came back laden. To all sides the jabber of voices ebbed and flowed.

"I interrupted you," Howard said.

"Oh, perhaps it's too complicated."

"Everything's complicated. The older you get the more complicated it becomes. What is it you were about to say?"

"How good it was when Ma was alive."

"Of course."

"That's all," Colin said. "Just that."

"Is it so bad for you now?"

"I wasn't thinking about myself."

Howard felt the telltale tug at the side of his mouth. He tried to shift his mind to where Colin wanted it to go, but Hampton Court was in the way, terrible little cameos. There was a time for the past, but it wasn't now, couldn't be now.

He said defensively: "You know I can't discuss my work, or my marriage, for that matter, but you shouldn't make the mistake—"

"I'm only interested in you."

"Thank you." Sharp again.

"When Ma was with us—"

"Not now." An enormous effort was required. The young could be so bloody cruel. "Please?"

"There wasn't so much hate in you then."

"Hate?"

"Correct."

Howard sucked in air. "That's up in lights as well—yes?"

"Among other things." Colin smiled affectionately: they

83

had shared so much. "Ma kept you on the rails, I reckon."

"Jesus Christ," Howard snorted at the ceiling. "You should have given warning you intended to preach."

"There's more."

"I don't think I want any more."

He forked too much into his mouth and choked, resentment burning him up. They were both silent, waves of other people's conversation breaking over them. And even then Chisholm was waiting in the wings of Howard's thoughts—Chisholm and Petrie and Leach, and question marks galore. There had to be some progress now. *Had* to be . . . Liverpool, the ferryboat, the Saladins, Hampton Court; Touchbutton had a list of credits to its name, over a hundred dead, while his own efforts seemed futile and unproductive, everything at a standstill.

Hate? He sat there with his eyes fixed on nothing in particular, the barmaids moving back and forth. The way Harriet had loved him was with a constant hope that he might somehow be changed without ceasing to be himself; made calmer, kinder, more patient, more tolerant. He knew without telling that she used to pray for this, kneeling there with him in the days when he went to Mass like clockwork, too. And it was part of her strength that she never failed him when he failed himself, part of her faith that what the world needed most would one day come to pass.

"Ma kept you on the rails, I reckon"—Colin's words reverberated. Nineteen; the nerve of it . . .

Yet in the same breath Howard was swept by the memory of the softness of Harriet's expression and the striving so often visible there and her warm urgent voice vibrant with love and worry.

A million times faster than speech he passed through this recollection of what once used to be, but the pain still lingered when the moment had gone. The sense of loss was like a yawning hole in the secret places of his heart. What he had lost was more than Harriet herself, but without her he hadn't the strength or the discipline to pull any of it back.

Hate? He wouldn't quibble. Ever since he'd witnessed what Touchbutton had done to the army wives and children on the ferryboat he had hated those responsible as if they were a single person.

Colin was saying: "Forgive me. I really turned the screw a bit."

Howard shrugged. "Better out than in, I suppose."

"All I'm saying, trying to say, is . . . is that I wish you'd take better care of yourself."

"Sure."

"I mean it. It's unfair to Eve, the way you are."

"Sure." He roused himself and glanced at his watch. There could be news from Chisholm soon. "I'm only sorry it's been so rushed." To be read like a book was disconcerting beyond words, but he couldn't believe Colin had met him merely for this one purpose. "Anything else up your sleeve?"

"Afraid so."

"Not along the same lines, I hope."

"It's a request."

Howard only needed a second or two. "Money?" He found a brief strained smile, which made him look older.

"Strictly a loan."

"How much?"

"Fifty pounds . . . A loan, mind. Three months at the outside."

Howard nodded. The generations didn't change.

"You'll have to come back to the office. I haven't got my checkbook with me and I don't carry that sort of cash."

"Okay."

They finished eating and left. Buckingham Gate was only around the corner. The sky was clearing but the streets were still wet, and people hurried, intent on their destinations.

"When d'you return to Bristol?"

"This afternoon."

"And when'll I see you again?"

"Before Christmas."

"At Christmas itself?"

"Possibly."

"Only possibly? Eve and I are pretty sure to be at home."

"I'll have to see. . . . I've been asked if I'd lend a hand with A.S.H."

"Which is what?"

"The Arundel Scheme for the Homeless."

"Oh, yes?" Howard wasn't really listening. Already, as they turned past the railings into the office entrance, his mind had got its blinkers on. Yet he could still manage a postscript. "Well, you're very welcome to come to us—you know that."

He led Colin along the third-floor corridor to the end office with its winter views over Wellington Barracks and the park beyond. He'd had to vouch for Colin's identity, signing a pass for the doorman. He gave it to Colin now, almost as if he realized he might forget.

"Here, you'll need this to get out."

Centered on his desk were two separate Manila folders. Standing against a chrome wind-on calendar was the photograph of Leach and Warrick. Howard picked up the folders with the eagerness of someone obsessed, the nervous tic dragging at his mouth as though he flinched from some secret pain.

Each contained a single sheet of paper with a timed and dated reference in the top right-hand corner. Both were headed MARTIN GRAHAM LEACH. The first was a month-by-month breakdown by Special Branch of Leach's points of call during his U.K. visits, July to October inclusive. They read as follows: *Odeon Cinema, Kensington High Street, 2; Albert Hall, 1; Blue Angel Restaurant, King's Road,*

Chelsea, 5; Golden Jacey's, St. Martin's Lane, 2; The Grapes, Hammersmith, 8; Green Lane, Bromley, 0.

Green Lane was where the mother lived. Otherwise there was nothing particularly significant. No stone unturned, though; that was clear. Disappointed, Howard glossed over the list and opened the second folder. It contained a Telex message from Petrie, and this time his heart leaped as he read.

"Da?"

He wasn't there.

"Da?" Colin said, still waiting by the door. "D'you think I could possibly have the check?"

Howard came back from a long way away. His lips had tightened and his eyes glittered. They seemed to have gone very, very dark. "Sure," he said. "Of course."

He sat down and wrote it out, scribbling. "All right?" he asked, holding it up for Colin to take. Hurry, hurry, get this over with; that's how it seemed. "Okay?"

"Thanks. Thanks very much . . . But it's a loan, mind."

Howard didn't reply. He'd gone back to the Telex already. Colin watched him, and for the second time that day what he saw urged him to risk a tone of gentle command.

"See a doctor, will you?"

Then the telephone buzzed and he knew it was useless to try any more.

📶 14

The call was from Chisholm, speaking from the brigadier's office in G.H.Q. Belfast and asking Howard to go on the scrambler.

"Well?"

"Got news for you, Duncan. We've run a few basic child's guide tests up to two thousand yards unimpeded vision, and it's been a lulu each time. On the other hand, if you deflect the signal by screening the detonator, then it's a dead duck. We used metal, ferrous metal. That's the first thing. Predictable, really, but even so—"

"When are you and Sheard coming back?"

"There's a flight in about an hour." He sounded close enough to have been in the next room, and Howard had never known him more enthusiastic. "We've also done some elementary dismantling and poking about."

"Tell me."

"Again, roughly what one might have expected. Ingenious, though. The detonator's incredibly engineered. Mallory battery, reed switches, narrow band frequency tuned oscillators—"

"How large?"

"Three inches by a half. We've no more than scratched the surface of its capability, but it does seem that other screening materials, nonmetallic, that is, don't have the same inhibiting effect."

The Hampton Court Touchbutton was under the Marines' bus, *under* it; the Saladins were picked off by charges buried at the roadside; Liverpool was a suitcase bomb. . . . As fast as light Howard weighed Chisholm's findings against the facts as he understood them to be. God knows about the ferryboat, but all the odds were that it was a suitcase job as well, several of them, four to five hundred pounds of explosive.

"Makes sense," he said.

Chisholm launched into further technicalities, but as far as Howard was concerned they could wait.

"Any ideas at all who produces 'em?"

"Not from what we've got here. But I can't help telling myself they're East German."

"Oh?"

"Maybe I'm wildly wrong, but I've suggested to Sheard that your department ought to investigate the experimental work done in this direction during the last decade by the D.D.R. . . . . Done commercially, understand?"

"Got you."

"I'll put all this in writing, Duncan. I'll let you have a copy of my preliminary report to the Minister just as soon as I can. . . . Tomorrow. A much fuller and more detailed paper will follow as soon as Weapons Co-ordination has carried out a complete assessment. Range and effectiveness of screening—natural and artificial—need to be thoroughly investigated."

"Philip."

"There's also the question of preventive jamming."

Chisholm started elaborating on bomb-disposal techniques and the possibility of the protection of bomb-disposal personnel. None of this was of more than academic interest to Howard, who sat hunched at his desk and told himself that, up to now, a Touchbutton charge had never been discovered in time to be disarmed. Indeed, Touchbutton's most sinister and horrific factor was that its operator could bide his time and choose his exact moment; and maximum damage and casualties went hand in hand with there being no warning.

"They'll be ramming them down our throats next," Chisholm had remarked after the Liverpool bomb. And, listening to him now, Howard was confirmed in the hardness of his heart that what was needed, first and foremost, was to track down the source and cut off supplies.

East Germany . . . His eyes were never still, flicking from the picture of Leach and Warrick to the Telex from Petrie. East Germany . . . Could be, could be. He gazed across the room at the wall map of Europe and swiftly traced an imaginary line between Warsaw and Rotterdam. Why's Leach the prime suspect? the Home Secretary had asked. "Because of the photograph?"

Yes. To begin with, yes. But now there was more.

"Philip," he cut in a second time.

"Yes?"

"Speak to me tomorrow, will you?"

"Very well."

"And tell young Sheard I'm expecting him in here later this afternoon."

"Will do . . . Bye."

Howard hung up. He crinkled his forehead, an awful throbbing there suddenly, and blinked at the breakdown of Leach's known movements in London. The chances were that somewhere among the list of places visited Leach kept a rendezvous. A contact was certain to exist; Howard was sure of it, increasingly sure, despite the fact that Special Branch's investigations had so far proved negative. To him it seemed inevitable: nobody operated without a local control. But how in the hell could those responsible check out every single individual Leach brushed shoulders with? There wasn't time, had never been time since he first saw the telltale picture of Leach and Warrick together at Galatorsko.

"Seems to me you're on dreadfully thin ice . . ."

Well, it wasn't so thin now. With a sense of incipient triumph Howard glanced at the Telex from Warsaw once again.

Subject has indicated ability to infiltrate associate into Ireland, the message read. *Progress at last—Petrie.*

15

Sheard's face was like a kid's. "One guess."

"John?" Carol went higher the second time. *"John?"*

"Listen, darling—"

"Where are you phoning from?"

"Belfast."

"Are you staying?"

"No, we're leaving in twenty minutes."

"Oh, *good* . . . So you'll be home tonight?"

"Late."

"Better late than not at all."

"We're at the airport," he told her. "Chisholm and me. And we're on the scheduled flight at fifteen thirty."

"Fifteen—?"

"Thirty. Half after three." The line clucked at them. "How've you been today?"

"Fine, absolutely fine."

"Sure?"

"Sure." She laughed happily. Idiot. "A couple of weeks from now it might be a different story, but right now everything's fine. So relax. Darling, you only left here this morning, and Belfast isn't exactly the other end of the world."

"Miss me?"

"Of course. How about you?"

"Always," he said. "See you."

One year married. Carol sounded a kiss for him as he put the phone down. He came away from the booth with a slightly faraway expression and crossed the concourse to where Chisholm was waiting. The brigadier had come to see them off, and Chisholm had the Touchbutton box looking totally innocuous in a plastic airline bag.

"All set?"

Sheard nodded. "Sorry. Didn't mean to keep you."

"You can board any time you like," the brigadier said, restless with his feet as usual. He spoke to Chisholm. "We've arranged for you to bypass the security checkpoint. The detector's got enough on its plate without your little load, wouldn't you say?" He creased his long totem-pole face into his own special version of a grin. "Any time. When it suits you."

Sheard picked up Chisholm's bag as well as his own; both had brought one in case of an overnight stay.

"Good-bye then," Chisholm said, offering a hand, "and thanks. Thanks a lot."

"Our pleasure, sir. Hope it's been worthwhile."

He led them past the queues, which were just beginning to move. A ground stewardess detached herself from the checkpoint and quickly examined their tickets and boarding cards.

"This way, gentlemen."

"Give my regards to London," the brigadier said in parting, as near to sounding wistful as he'd ever allowed himself.

They followed the peaches-and-cream stewardess down the ramp and across the apron to where the Trident stood waiting. The breeze that had plagued them out on the firing range found them again, and they walked with their heads turned slightly to one side, eyes narrowed and watering. How the stewardess could somehow maintain her lacquered look and also manage a pleasant smile was a mystery to them both.

Chisholm went first up the steps and into the empty plane. "Anywhere?" he asked.

"I'm not particular."

He chose a row on the starboard side just aft the wing. The bags Sheard shoved under their feet, and Chisholm sat with the Touchbutton package on his lap, as protective of it as a miser.

"D'you smoke?"

"No, thanks."

He lit a cigarette and settled back. "I told Duncan Howard I'd be letting him have a sight of my preliminary report just as soon as possible, and you'll be with him by this evening. So—between us—I don't think he can feel neglected."

The other passengers began to file aboard, men mostly, executives, salesmen, the boom years showing in their faces, expense-account lunches still strong on their breath.

"Got any questions?" Chisholm said.

"Not really. Nothing technical, anyhow." Sheard shook his head. "In other directions, ah, that's another matter."

"Must say I don't envy your department its job. So often, it seems to me, you're expected to make something out of nothing."

"That's right."

"Bricks without straw." Chisholm tapped the package gently. "Not like this. Before the week's done we'll know exactly where we stand, thank God."

The breeze had left a glow on their faces. The steps were pulled away and the door sealed; the warning lights showed, and people clipped the safety belts around them.

"No smoking, sir," a passing stewardess told Chisholm with a carbon-copy smile. "Later, yes, but not now."

"Incredible, isn't it?" Chisholm grumbled to Sheard alongside. "That kind of thing always make me feel like a naughty boy. . . . At my age, too."

But he obeyed. He sat there with the Touchbutton

93

secure in his lap, nursing it as the aircraft trundled to the far end of the dispatch runway.

"How long've you been with Duncan Howard?"

"Eighteen months."

"Great guy," Chisholm said. "A real beaver. Puts in far more than he ever takes out. More than's good for him sometimes."

The Trident braked and powered around until it pointed down the long smeared runway. At exactly three-thirty-six the whine of the engines rose to a scream and the plane began to hurtle forward. As it lifted off, smooth and graceful in its sudden buoyancy, the feeling of thrust diminished. The green earth to either side fell rapidly away. Second by second the horizon widened. Sixty-five minutes from now and they'd be coming in to land at Heathrow.

"Another thing about Duncan," Chisholm said, picking up where he'd left off. "If *he* can't get to the bottom of this bloody Touchbutton thing—"

The plane disintegrated then. Nobody aboard lived a heartbeat longer. Nobody survived to describe what that cataclysmic microsecond was like. But a man in a field directly below said later that it looked as if a violent red-and-yellow hole had suddenly been punched in the sky.

Without warning.

Then all the pieces had started raining down, in silence and slow motion.

🛜 16

"What height was the Trident?"

"Two thousand."

In anguish Howard began to repeat himself. "And no survivors?"

"None."

"Oh, Jesus." He closed his eyes, crushed by the shock, a remnant of disbelief still beating fists of protest against his senses.

None . . . Not one.

"Sixty-three on board." The Home Secretary's voice was like a knife in the brain. "Sixty-three total, passengers and crew."

"How long ago was this?"

"Forty minutes or so . . . It blew up, Howard. There was a midair explosion shortly after take-off. Nobody had a chance."

Yes, yes.

Even so, Howard clutched at a straw. "Are you certain Chisholm took this flight? Isn't it possible—?"

"My information is adamant that he was a passenger."

Oh, Jesus, Howard thought frantically. Philip Chisholm and John Sheard. Sixty-three dead, but his mind was tight around only two. Others could grieve about the rest, others must come to terms with what this meant to them.

"There's been a Touchbutton claim."

"No!"

"The report's in front of me."

"But that's crazy. One of the facts to come out of the range tests this morning was the thing's ineffectiveness when the charge was screened with metal. Chisholm told me so himself."

"Nevertheless, the claim's been made."

"Then it's a lie. Chisholm didn't make that kind of mistake." *Didn't*, he'd said; the tense had changed already.

"How in God's name does it matter now?"

"It matters," Howard snapped back: he would be loyal to the last. He managed to separate a part of his mind from its stupefaction. "They'd have gone for the Trident because Chisholm had a Touchbutton with him. *Because* of that, d'you see? But they couldn't have used one to blow it up."

"All right, all ri—"

"They'd have been forced to employ a conventional device. There's no other way. And when everything's been sifted through and checks have been made on how the plane was loaded and whether all the baggage was satisfactorily security-examined, then you'll find that Philip Chisholm wasn't wrong."

Howard's face was damp with sweat, cold with it.

"Don't try to tell me we should play Touchbutton down," the Home Secretary started angrily. "You of all people."

"I'm doing no such thing."

"They'll be holding us to ransom unless we can put a stop to outrages like this."

"Do you suppose I don't know that?" Howard flared. Words, bloody clichés, always the same. "Listen . . . No, *you* listen. This wasn't chance. This wasn't coincidence. They didn't especially want a Trident with sixty-odd people. They didn't especially want Philip Chisholm either. Or a young man from this department who'd gone along as an observer."

His voice shook.

"What they *did* want was the one Touchbutton set in our possession. Why? So that Weapons Co-ordination wouldn't have time to learn all there is to learn and for us maybe to pick up a clue as to where it's manufactured . . . *That's* why they've gone to these lengths. Not merely as a demonstration of power. And if you seriously believe that I'm in some way anxious to minimize or decry the Touchbutton campaign, then you'd better suggest that I be relieved of my departmental responsibilities here and now."

He flung the phone down, heartbreak and a sense of impotence terribly compounded. He covered his face with his hands for a moment, distressed as never before, taunted by one particular recollection as his mind thrashed in all directions. "Come and have a look at what sort of toy we've laid our hands on"—Chisholm on the line at half past four in the morning, *this* morning, a suggestion that had prompted his own call to Sheard minutes later, telling him to be at Heathrow in time for the nine o'clock to Belfast.

For what? he thought. To show willingness, to keep the department generally in the picture; no more than that. Any other hour of the day and he might well have declined. He could still hear Carol's sleepy "Hello, who is it?" when she fumbled the receiver off the rest. Only this morning. "John, it's for you. It's Mr. Howard. . . ."

He sat there, swamped by it all. Chisholm as well as Sheard. And all the others. Hate swelled, and he let it fester, drawing on it to extinguish grief and guilt. Then the phone buzzed and he found he'd picked it up.

"Yes?"

The Home Secretary. Back again and alarmed enough to be apologizing. "The last thing I want is for you and me to be at each other's throats, Howard. But we have to square up to the facts, which means we can't simply sit around and wait for the next Touchbutton to bring terror and havoc—"

"Nobody's sitting around."

"Of course not."

Howard couldn't stop himself. "Chisholm wasn't sitting around, Sheard wasn't—"

"I'm talking about *now*. What we do now and in the

97

immediate future—Special Branch, the Irish Section, Weapons Co-ordination, the Bomb Squad, everybody concerned. I propose calling a meeting, here, in my office, at the earliest possible opportunity in order to draw up a concerted emergency policy. . . ."

Howard listened, only a part of his mind thawed out. He glanced repeatedly at the photograph of Leach as he listened, Leach and Warrick at Galatorsko, the blue-green pool and the tree-clad hills beyond the rosebushes and surrounding shrubbery. And each time he felt an urge like lust, ugly and savage, demanding satisfaction.

"The more Touchbutton they can stockpile, the bolder and more extreme they are likely to become. . . ."

They.

Howard shifted position. Vaughan tapped at the door and entered. He waited uncertainly for a moment, pale and disturbed, then withdrew. He must have heard the news; everyone in the outer office would have heard by now. They, the Home Secretary was saying. *They . . .*

"I doubt whether I can get you all together before tomorrow morning, so I'd like you to earmark the afternoon."

"I won't be here," Howard said.

"Your contribution will be all-important."

"I'll be in Warsaw."

There was a slight pause. "I didn't know about this." The Home Secretary got no response. "I didn't know about this, Howard," he repeated with some petulance. "You made no mention of it this morning. Only a few hours ago you were arguing a convincing case for not closing in too soon."

"This won't be too soon."

"What have you got in mind?"

"Using somebody."

"Leach?"

"Martin Graham Leach." Howard measured out the name. "I can't function at arm's length any more."

The slow hiss of indrawn breath raced along the wire.

"It's all very well, this sudden switch of yours, but what are you actually proposing?"

"To start with," Howard gritted, "I'm going to scare the shit out of him."

"And then?"

"See where he runs. Where and who to."

Others—north and south of the border—could apply their minds and energies to Nolan. But Leach would have a contact nearer home than him. There had to be a London link, and loss of nerve could bring about the giveaway.

"And if he doesn't scare?"

"He'll scare, all right. Fear's the best weapon there is."

"Doesn't run? Doesn't lead you anywhere?"

Only cautious men asked questions like that, men who put their reputations first, men without hearts to wear on their sleeves.

"I'm not waiting any longer," Howard parried.

He left a lot of things unsaid, sick in the stomach from shock and blinkered by the fierceness of his intent. He hung up eventually, no proper recollection afterward of what else he'd told the Home Secretary. The decision to act had come off the top of his head, yet he saw the essentials clearly. He wasn't a desk man, least of all now.

He buzzed the outer office. "Vaughan? Come in, would you please?" And when Vaughan arrived he said: "Have you heard?"

"It's unbelievable, absolutely unbelievable." Vaughan's expression said that death came to strangers, never to anyone you knew. "We're all sort of numb out there."

"Naturally."

When Harriet died, old Father Cash had talked at length about God in His loving mercy, but all Howard could think about now was vengeance. There was a rage inside him still, and he nursed it.

"On top of everything," Vaughan said, "Carol's expecting a baby soon."

99

The muscle at the corner of Howard's mouth went twitch, twitch, in rapid succession. He hadn't forgotten.

"One of the things I want from you is her address. The others are an airline ticket to Warsaw for tomorrow, and—" Howard fished his passport and some photograph spares from a side drawer—"a visa. I don't know what problems and delays there are over obtaining Polish visas, but pull out all the stops and get me one quick. I want to fly before noon if I can."

"I'll do my best." Vaughan nodded, not used to this.

"Then Telex Petrie and tell him I'm coming. Give him my flight number and ask him to meet me."

"Very well."

Howard jerked a glance at his watch. Four-twenty-eight. Chisholm and Sheard had been dead for almost an hour, but time had changed its measure. Already the day seemed everlasting, the pattern of it blurred.

"There's something else," Vaughan said. "A message from your wife."

"Oh, yes?"

"She asked me to ask you if you would be going to the Diadem tonight."

"The Diadem?" Howard's head was splitting and he couldn't cope with normality.

"And would you please let her know as early as possible."

"What time was this?"

"About half past two."

It was in one ear and out the other. He switched on some lights and flipped through what little there was awaiting his attention, initialing everything he read, unable to concentrate. After a while Vaughan came back with Carol Sheard's address: Hall Road, Maida Vale. For several minutes the slip of paper lay on Howard's desk, unsettling him further, and finally he got up and put on his coat.

But for him, Sheard would still be alive.

All he took from his desk were the address and the photograph of Leach and Warrick.

But for him, but for them.

A trace of disbelief revived for a second or two when he saw Sheard's name in the corridor: MR. JOHN SHEARD, ASSISTANT TO THE DIRECTOR. It made him burn. Sheard *and* Chisholm . . . He opened the door of the general office and put his head and shoulders inside. Vaughan was a couple of desks away, and he called across curtly to say that he was leaving.

"Very good, Mr. Howard."

"Contact me the moment you know what flight I can take tomorrow. And then be at Heathrow with my papers."

"Right."

Howard took the lift down. It was quite dark outside. He walked to where the car was parked with his hands thrust deep into his pockets. There was a chill in the air, but he didn't notice. "As I live and breathe, we'll get whoever's responsible"—when he reached Carol's that's what he would say. Others would comfort and sustain her, but he alone could promise that.

He clipped the seat belt across him and drove to Hyde Park Corner, survived the whirling melee there and made his way through the park to Marble Arch and into the Edgware Road. He drove like an automaton, scores of private images overprinting his natural vision, oblivious of the hornblast and a whinnying screech of brakes right on his tail at Tyburn Way.

Hall Road showed itself obediently less than fifteen minutes after his leaving Buckingham Gate, but the Victorian mansion flat he was after did no such thing. In the end he parked in an empty meter space, to go searching on foot. And eventually he discovered it—a ground-floor apartment with a side entrance and a flagstone path leading between waist-high shrubbery to a brightly lit front door.

101

Howard braced himself before ringing the bell, matching his own distress to the grief he would find. God knows who would be with Carol or how well she would have held together. In the very moment of the bell sounding he was terribly conscious of how little he knew about her, how little he'd known about Sheard himself. At best, your junior colleagues were acquaintances.

Through the crinkled glass of the door he watched the initial smudge of movement tighten into the shape of a woman. Yellow dress, long dark hair. Then the latch clicked and the door opened. Carol Sheard stood peering out, enormously swollen in her pregnancy, and for a split second Howard didn't recognize her.

"Oh, it's you, Mr. Howard."

His scalp seemed to shrink. *She didn't know.* She smiled at him happily, a bright plump smile.

"John isn't back from Belfast—"

Two hours gone by and she still didn't know.

"He rang to say he'd be late, you see. But do come in, please come in . . ."

Howard stepped woodenly inside, appalled and unprepared.

 **17**

In the early days of his coming to Warsaw, during the empty time before Anna when Saxon Engineering was the be-all and end-all of his existence, Leach would sometimes pick up a woman and take her to his room at the Forum. He looked upon the hotel as his base, and in that sense Anna had changed nothing. He still dealt with his correspondence there, wrote his reports for Saxon there, entertained the occasional client there. A base was essential, and, though he no longer slept at the hotel, he regularly used whichever room he was allocated.

Now, in the early evening, he finished fixing his tie and hauled his jacket on. In half an hour he was due back at Anna's, and he knew what awaited him, what she expected of him, what Retman's inflexibility threatened to make impossible. Night long they'd talk about it, lies and half-lies woven into so much of what he would be forced to say.

On the bed was a copy of the London *Daily Express*—today's edition. Leach had found it in the hotel's foyer, presumably discarded by someone who had just flown in, and the morning headlines seemed directed at him.

TOUCHBUTTON BLITZ CONTINUES, he read. HEAVY CASUALTIES AND DAMAGE.

His eyes swept the front page. The pictures he ignored, deliberately ignored, squeamish of what he guessed was in them. Since June a part of him had been uneasy, but never more than now. The campaign had scarcely begun—Retman had said as much—and by the time next May came around the monthly deliveries would have placed a massive destructive power into the hands of those who would use it.

Special Branch carried out a series of raids during the night and more than twenty people have been held for questioning. Some of the raids were in connection with the so-called Touchbutton bombings. . . .

Leach tossed the newspaper down. Boxes, Warrick had called them, but there was a limit to the extent that he could shut his mind. Little eddies of fear increasingly disturbed his calm. He was losing his taste for the money and the risks it paid for. Besides, there was something else he wanted now. All his life he had longed for love and never found it. Until now, until Anna. Sometimes, in her presence, he seemed closest to what he had always hoped he might become, and the future held out promises that were

103

more desirable than anything he had ever dreamed likely.

As soon as practicable he would finish with Warrick, break with Retman. There would be ten deliveries, and then no more. He would quit Saxon, too. Others had changed direction and so could he. For safety's sake a time would come when there must be no coming back to Poland and elsewhere, no retracing steps. He would vanish as Anna would vanish, change names as Anna would change names, begin again as Anna would begin again.

It was possible. Everything was possible. Ten thousand pounds in Switzerland; they wouldn't starve. Warrick had bought him and Retman had used him—okay. And he would see his contract through, vulnerable though it made him, because to break it now would be to bring disaster snarling at his heels. But, after that—nothing. Everything would diminish, ripples from a dying wave, diminish and recede.

He took the lift to the ground floor and crossed the echoing foyer. Muffled against the cold he waited outside for a taxi, third in line, the rumble of Warsaw all around.

"Where to?" the driver asked over one shoulder, and Leach told him, clumsy with the consonants.

"You American?" This in English.

"*Angielski.*"

"You have dollars?"

"No dollars."

"Pounds? . . . I give good price for pounds."

"I have no pounds," Leach said firmly.

He kept clear of the black market. It was commonly known that some of those who touted for foreign money were informers, in the pay of the police, and he wanted no trouble, no complications. There were dangers enough without the small temptations.

"I give more than two hundred for the pound," the driver persisted, unwilling to let go.

"Sorry—no pounds, no dollars."

Leach leaned back and watched the Warsaw night slide and wheel and turn. The lights were everywhere very bright in the crisp cold, and the people on the busy sidewalks moved with purpose. Away from the main thoroughfares the traffic thinned. He paid the taxi off three hundred meters from Anna's block and walked the rest of the way, in and out of the shadows, hearing the sound of his own footsteps, an element of prudence about his approach, cautious for Anna's sake, so different from the times he went to meet Retman or his appointed contact in London. He sweated then, uneasy, especially uneasy in London, clammy tentacles around his heart in case he was followed, never quite sure.

Six months from now all that would be done with; one year from now he would never even half expect a tap on his arm from behind. "Mr. Leach?" For weeks he'd wondered if it might come.

He turned into the entrance, almost no one about, and walked up the two flights—stone stairs, badly lit, three apartments to each floor, nothing to redeem the uncarpeted drabness of each landing.

"Hi."

He was inside quickly, into the small hall with its plain walls and the decorative posters and the dark place where coats were hung. Leach kissed Anna the moment the door was shut, a lover's kiss, holding her close, safe with her.

"You're early."

"Is that bad?"

"I am still cooking. Nothing is ready yet."

"There's no hurry."

He followed Anna into the kitchen. She looked tired, he thought, a little drawn, as if the day's disappointment had drained her. He poured some vodka for them both and opened one of the bottles of Hungarian red wine he had brought to the apartment on previous occasions.

"*Zdrowie pani.*" He raised his glass. "Here's to you."

"To us, Martin."

"To us as well."

He watched her while she busied herself at the stove. They had come a long, long way since that first chance meeting back in July, and swiftly, too.

"Soup to begin with—yes?"

"Great."

"Pea soup . . . *Grochowka*."

She glanced up searchingly, green eyes quivering, eager despite the setback. Whatever else, she was nothing if not resilient.

"When you said Ireland—" she began, then waited fractionally.

"How d'you mean?" It was as though there had been no afternoon's separation, nothing else on her mind in between.

"When you mentioned Ireland, getting me into Ireland . . . Would you come, too?"

"No."

"Where would you go?"

"To London. To my work, Anna. I've no choice about that."

She frowned. "And how long would I be in Ireland?"

"A week or so."

"Where would I live?"

"With friends."

"Your friends?"

"People I know, yes. But temporarily. Very, very temporarily."

As if with relief she clattered some dishes in the sink. "From Ireland I would go on to England?"

"That's right."

"Openly? With a passport?"

"That's right." Leach nodded. "Someone I know in London can help us there."

Her lips curled. "The 'someones' you know . . . Now, come and eat."

They sat at the table in the alcove, the curtains drawn, music from London softly on the radio. He'd already explained about the powerboat out of Rotterdam, the mid-Channel rendezvous and transshipment, the fishing yawl that would beach her on the Wexford coast, explained it without going into detail, speaking as if he were on the outer fringes of whatever might be possible. And she hadn't pressed for more than the bare essentials, hadn't questioned him in any depth. How he knew about these things, how he knew about such people—none of this apparently concerned her. All she hungered after was escape, a way through the wood, a time when here and now would cease to matter.

"This is truth, isn't it? Truth, Martin, every word?" That was about the most she'd said, and he'd managed to smooth the question marks away. Truth was made true by events.

He refilled his glass and drank. To hell with Retman, to hell with Warrick, to hell with falling down on a single month's delivery. The vodka stiffened him, emboldened him, but only on the surface of his will; underneath he was resigned. Anna and he would have to wait until next summer. June; it would have to be June. There were no alternatives. He had sold himself until then, a single handshake at Galatorsko more binding than anything written down. And it frightened him now, day by day a little more.

"Were you ever in Ireland yourself?"

"Once," Leach said.

"Long ago?"

"Last year."

The suck and crump and hiss of the waves on a moonless midnight beach were at the very center of his memory. For two hours he was there, two hours in Ireland, Nolan there with him while the load was brought ashore, Brendan Nolan, Nolan who'd come in person to give the password and verify Leach's credentials. "The first run you will make yourself—all the way," Warrick had instructed. "After that it will not be necessary."

"Only once?" Anna asked.

"That's all." To commit him, to involve him to the hilt: hindsight underlined the hold they had. "Once is enough."

"Didn't you like Ireland, Martin?"

"No."

Leach ate, imagination telescoping the future. Like Anna, he wanted to escape. Like her, he wanted the break to be soon; sooner than soon. She smiled at him across the table, the soup finished, a dish of *bigos* in front of them now. They were allies, conspirators, sustained by a need for each other: he saw the look in her eyes, the hope and the anxiety, and he longed to be done with pretense.

"Tell me about London," she said. "Would we stay in London?"

"It depends." He was guarded. "We'll have to see."

"I know so little about everything over there."

He leaned across and kissed her. The music ended as their lips touched.

"*A British Airways Trident was this afternoon blown up soon after taking off from Belfast on a scheduled flight to London. . . .*"

The voice found him, singling him out from eight hundred miles away. Even here, even now.

"*A total of sixty-three people were killed. There were no survivors, and wreckage was scattered over a wide area, some of it narrowly missing a housing estate. . . .*"

Leach closed his eyes as he held the kiss.

"*Shortly after the explosion a claim was made that this was yet another Touchbutton attack, and indeed it bears all the hallmarks of this new weapon. . . .*"

Boxes, Warrick had called them. But it was too late now for crocodile tears.

🎵 18

Eve's first words to Howard were: "Where on *earth* have you been?"

"I went to see Sheard's wife." Widow, *widow*: it beat in his brain.

"Didn't you get my message?"

"No," he said. "What message?" Then: "Oh, yes . . . That."

"I particularly asked you to let me know in good time."

They were in the hall, Howard hardly through the front door, Eve holding the glass of sherry she'd emerged with from the sitting room.

"Time for what?" He put his briefcase down and walked past her, still with his coat on. "I went to see Sheard's wife."

"I don't understand."

"Someone had to do it."

"You normally call if you're going to be late. In any case. And today I particularly asked—"

"I forgot," Howard said, making for the drinks tray. "Vaughan gave me the message, but I forgot."

"That's nice to know." Eve's look was withering. "Oh, isn't that nice."

"I'm sorry."

"You're making a habit of being that."

The ice cracked in the glass, snap-snap, as the whiskey flooded in.

Eve went on: "You'd suggested going to the Diadem, remember? Yesterday. It was *your* suggestion, after all. But—hell—look what time it is."

Howard clenched his jaws. With disbelief he said: "Don't you know what's happened?"

"It's too late for the Diadem now."

"For the love of Christ," he exploded. Sixty-three dead,

109

and no one bloody knew. Not even Carol had known. *"Haven't you heard, either?"*

The rage in his voice startled Eve. She turned her head sharply. A little time went by before she spoke. "The plane, you mean?"

"Philip Chisholm was on it."

"Oh, *no.*"

"*And* young Sheard."

"I . . . I had no idea."

"Well, you have now." He drank, and felt the bite. "You have now."

"D'you mean they've been killed?" It was Eve's turn to look incredulous.

"Killed, yes. That's why—"

"But the office didn't say anything. The person I spoke to—Vaughan, is it?—he didn't mention this."

"You called before it had happened."

"There was something on the news at six. About the crash. I was having a bath and I caught it on the radio. But I never connected it with—"

"It wasn't a crash. It was Touchbutton." Howard lifted his glass again, haunted by the awful way Carol's eyes had gone dead at the center.

"Touchbutton," he repeated. "Mine."

Other men came home and talked about the cars they'd sold or the new accounts they'd got hold of or the deals they'd pulled off for themselves or their clients. No war for them in the midst of peace and plenty, no colleagues murdered, no drive for revenge aching like cancer. Another day tomorrow, and, fine, why not the Diadem tonight after all?

"Was Philip married?"

"No. But Sheard was. And when I got there—"

Howard let a gesture finish for him. He'd been so cruelly unprepared, so clumsy, so bad, so desperately bad: and even when the doctor arrived, and others, too—an aunt

110

and a woman neighbor and a grim-faced father-in-law—he hadn't been much use to anyone. He'd never been able to handle tears. Or find them, either.

"I'm flying to Warsaw tomorrow."

"Oh?"

"Around midday, I hope."

"For how long?"

"Can't say." Howard's mouth twitched like plucked elastic. "I'm going to nail these bastards."

"D'you mean to say you know who's responsible?"

"Think so."

"Only 'think'?"

"More than just that."

"In Warsaw?"

He nodded, coat still on, glass already empty. Petrie's evidence was building up at last, tape by tape.

"Can you touch them there?"

"After a fashion." Leach was an instrument about to be put to practical use.

"How?"

Other men came home and used their wives as an audience. But Howard didn't. Not with Eve. With Harriet, yes. Harriet had always listened, been ready to listen, guided him, calmed him. These days, though, he felt separated from the meanings of things as they had once been. Harriet would have somehow found a formula to ease the hatred out of him, allowed him to think straight, to reason better. Harriet wouldn't have made him feel so lonely or the silences so brittle.

He said: "You know I can't go into details."

"Which means you expect me to decipher riddles."

"Rubbish."

He gave himself another Scotch and crossed to the phone. Dekker, he wanted a journalist named Dekker. Eve watched him, displeased at being shut out, on edge because of his lateness, grieved by the news—all three: and anxious, not

111

liking what she saw about him. Everyone changed, but most people learned to change together. It was never to have been like this.

"All I was about to say—"

"Hold it, will you?" He started dialing.

"Why not now? When will there be another chance?"

Howard waited, looking away, listening to the ringing tone.

"What's happening to you, for God's sake?" Eve spread her hands. "What's taken possession—?"

"Steven?"

She tossed her head despairingly and started out of the room.

"Steven, it's Duncan. Duncan Howard . . . Yes, yes. Oh, sure . . . Have I caught you at a bad moment? . . . Good . . . Well, yes, there's something I badly want to discuss and I can't do it over an open line. Can I meet you tomorrow first thing? I'm flying out of the country later in the day, so it'll have to be in the morning. . . . Good, great, that'll be fine. Nine-thirty, at your place . . . Thanks."

He hung up and walked through into the kitchen. Eve was there and she could feel his will, his obsession, restless and relentless, like a current about her.

She said: "This has become a vendetta for you, hasn't it?"

It was phrased like a question but stated as a fact. Howard didn't answer. He ran the cold tap and splashed some water into the whiskey. Eve waited a few seconds, then spoke again, aiming to bridge the gap.

"Is that the Dekker I think it is? Quite often on TV?"

"That's the one."

"Where does he live?"

"Hurlingham."

"And you'll go on from there to Heathrow?"

"Yes."

She glanced at the clock: it showed nine. For a few moments she didn't seem to know what else to say.

112

"So what are we going to do?"

"Huh?"

Eve made a small movement of defeat. "Now . . . about eating."

Howard came back from a long way away. As if for the first time, he saw what Eve was wearing—the long skirt, the silvered blouse, the dress earrings. An enormous effort was required to surmount the stab of resentment her appearance caused him. So poised, so attractive: it made him feel old.

"We could go down the hill into Kingston."

"I don't mind."

"There's that Italian place."

"I don't mind," she said flatly.

The garage doors were still open, the Granada's engine warm. Howard's eyes glittered savagely as he drove. Again there was the pain in his head. "Take care of yourself, Duncan," Chisholm had joked as they parted at Fisher's. "There aren't too many of us left."

Well, Leach was left: Howard felt his hatred rise like bile. It had to be Leach. *Had to be.* The tapes and the photograph put two and two together, but discovering Leach's London contact was only part of the plan, no longer enough. Howard had gone past that. He wanted Leach to bleed, bleed inside with what he'd done. He wanted him self-confessed, on a plate. Personally.

They were shown to a table. They drank the wine and ate the food and listened to the music. They were like strangers, few words, hardly a glance exchanged. People came and went, and eventually they went as well. They crossed to where Howard had parked the car and got in. And after the doors were slammed to, in the silence as Howard was reaching for the ignition, Eve touched him on the arm.

"Listen, Duncan." Her voice was low and grave, with an intensity he never forgot. "Philip Chisholm was your friend —I know that. John Sheard was your colleague—I know

113

that, too. I didn't know them like you, of course, yet I grieve for them myself." Some oncoming headlights swept them. Eve closed her eyes and waited. Then she said: "But they're dead. Duncan. Dead . . . Whereas I'm your wife and I'm alive."

She cleared her throat, as if the hurt was choking her.

"Take me home, please."

📶 19

The fawn-colored Morris Marina ran onto the hard shoulder of the M6 motorway at precisely three minutes to twelve. It came to rest at the side of the northbound lane two hundred yards from Exit 13. Motorists who remembered seeing it reported afterwards that two men were with the car. Most of them recalled that, to begin with, the hood was stuck up in the air and one of the men, head well down, seemed to be tinkering with the engine, trying to fix something. Several people reported seeing one of the men walking back along the verge, presumably having made an emergency telephone call. But nobody was able to say with any certainty what either of the men looked like, and no one was able to give the car's number.

It stayed on the shoulder for twenty-four minutes. During the last six of these the hood was dropped down, and both men got into the car and waited, the one in the passenger seat with his ear pressed to the radio telephone built into the glove pocket.

Eventually he started getting the information that mattered, crucial information.

"Immediately behind a white Freezeezy van . . . Fifty

to sixty yards behind white van and already pulled into slow lane preparing to exit . . . Quarter of a mile to go . . ."

It was a sharp, meticulous, confident voice.

"Three hundred yards to go, indicator already signaling . . . From now on take it visually. Black Daimler about to pass your position . . ."

The Freezeezy van cruised by. Both men tensed, crouching a little. The Prime Minister's Daimler followed, with a rubbery whoosh of tires. As it did so the man behind the wheel of the Marina pushed the offside door wide and leaned out, clear of all obstruction. Seven seconds later he pressed the keys of the Touchbutton he was holding and the bomb planted at the roadside detonated with a flashing spurt of flame.

The blast rocked the Marina from end to end before it lurched forward. A wheel severed from what remained of the Daimler was still spinning like a coin as the Marina scorched past, jarring through the gears into the night.

Leach lay with Anna in the small soft bed in her apartment, midnight now, the dyspeptic rumble of Warsaw's traffic all but finished until another winter's dawn discolored the sky. A little snow had started powdering down.

Tired though he was he couldn't sleep. His body ached from loving her, but his brain was on a treadmill and wouldn't let him go. An hour after Anna had drifted into sleep herself he was smoking his third cigarette and staring at the ceiling, watching the smoke curdle as it rose through the moonlight that slanted in bars through the windows.

The world got smaller every day, but only for some.

He must speak with Retman again. One more try. Not tomorrow, he couldn't tomorrow, but the next day. In any case, before he left for Leipzig on Friday. Somehow Retman had to be made to believe that Saxon was continuing to press about the obsolescent stock and its removal. Once Retman accepted that—no matter how reluctantly—and gave the okay to there being no load carried in December, once that happened, then the chance was there, and they were over the first hurdle. The first and the most dangerous. The others could be fixed—Rotterdam, Wexford, London; money could produce what was wanted. But Retman had to be persuaded, convinced, no suspicion aroused. Above all no suspicion aroused.

Leach streamed a jet of smoke nervously from his mouth and stubbed the cigarette in the ashtray on the floor beside the bed.

How? . . . How?

He was never less than uneasy with Retman. Demanding Warrick's intervention was a bluff and Retman knew it, had showed that he knew it. Retman never got excited and never became angry. He stayed detached, using the human machinery Warrick had given him, making sure it worked to the agreed level of efficiency. Leach pictured the podgy face, the constipated pallor, the red-rimmed eyes. To be uneasy was one thing, to be scared was another. And he was scared now, scared of Retman finding out what he was planning.

"You are sweating, my friend, did you know?"

Leach closed his eyes. Anna was breathing to a steady rhythm, and he envied her. He turned sideways and tried in vain to stop his mind in its tracks.

Retman. He must speak to Retman. Either he must try with Retman once again or they must wait until next summer. And life was too short for that, Anna had kept saying, loving him and holding him close.

The fire in the Redway Furniture warehouse in Birmingham was started by an incendiary. There was no way of knowing this at the time, no way of being sure of anything except the speed at which the fire took hold and engulfed at least a third of the huge building within the first half hour. The stink of burning was everywhere, and the roar of it was like a wind.

By three o'clock there were eighteen pumpers and engines at the scene, seven slender turntable ladders poking high into the garish sky, two entire streets awash and strewn with crisscrossed hoses, police cars positioned to isolate the whole area, scores of helmeted men silhouetted against the flames, ambulances waiting as close as the chaos allowed.

And at five past three a solitary Touchbutton operator, watching from a window almost half a mile away, decided the concentration of manpower was then at its maximum, and blew the planted charge.

"Harriet?"

Eve stirred, barely conscious yet just sufficiently alerted.

"Harriet?" Howard mumbled again, the muscles of his jaws working as he slept.

God knows where his mind had taken him. She lay still and listened, blinking as if to wipe out the dark; but no more came from his lips, and in the long silence something inside Eve seemed to shrivel away to nothing. She clenched her hands and bit on her lower lip, as if by doing these things she might manage to keep the tears at bay.

"Yes?" the Home Secretary said, his sleep broken for the third time. "Right. Put him through."

He listened, propped on one elbow. First the attack on the Prime Minister's car, then the Birmingham fire blast, now an incomplete flash about an explosion at Nine Elms, London's new Covent Garden.

"How long ago?" His bedside clock was showing five-twenty-five. "Right," he said. "Well, I'll go over there straight away. Ten minutes and I'll be ready, so let me have a car as soon as possible."

He hung up and swung his thin legs urgently out of bed. The Prime Minister hadn't been in the Daimler, but the driver and a detective had died. Fourteen firemen were killed in Birmingham, and how many deaths there'd been at Nine Elms wasn't yet known. But one thing was clear. Nowhere was safe any more. Yesterday the Trident. And now three separate incidents, audacious and terrifying, all in a single night.

Howard hadn't been far wrong. There was a war on, and they were losing it.

 **20**

Howard spent an hour with Steven Dekker.

Twice in that hour he rang Buckingham Gate, but Vaughan wasn't back from the Polish Consulate. Howard swore, never still, watching the time. It was approaching half past ten before Vaughan came through to say that he'd obtained the visa and booked Howard on a British Airways flight out of Heathrow at twelve-fifteen.

"Don't forget to advise Petrie."

"It's already done."

"I'll see you at Heathrow, then. Eleven-thirty."

At that point Dekker started dotting i's and crossing t's. "This'll happen tomorrow?"

"Unless everything misfires." He'd been told enough and no more.

"May I see the photograph of Warrick again?"

Howard showed it to him. Dekker studied it carefully. He was a large man, with a deceptively amiable manner. His face was deeply lined, the skin leathery, the bald head freckled: he looked younger on television than in the flesh.

"How old did you say Warrick is?"

"Thirty-six."

"Any special mannerisms I ought to be aware of?"

"Not that I know of."

"Does he smoke? Drink?"

"I'll get Vaughan to give you a note of everything relevant in the file."

"Fine. Well, I'll keep my fingers crossed and do the very best I can."

"Thanks, Steve."

Dekker eyed him critically, aware more than most how a course of action could damage or fulfill a man. They'd been acquaintances for years, and he didn't remember ever seeing Howard so strained or on edge. Impatient, wanting to be gone, an almost fanatical relentlessness in his burning gaze. Whatever else happened, he wouldn't compromise, wouldn't be deflected. It all showed—the nerves, the pressure, the fatigue, everything. And the driving ruthlessness.

"When did you last play cat-and-mouse?"

"It's been quite a while." A spasm distorted Howard's mouth. "But never like this. This time the claws are out."

"I can see that." Dekker nodded. At the door he said, with meaning: "Don't scratch too many people, Duncan." And Howard gave him a sharp bloodshot look, as if he'd intruded.

"Good-bye, Steve."

Howard drove to Heathrow and parked the Granada on one of the lower levels. Security was exceptionally tight and everything took longer as a consequence. Vaughan was waiting for him by the flight departure board, as arranged, and Howard instructed him hastily about supplying Dekker with the information he required, and dealing with various other matters that might need attention during his absence. Vaughan seemed to have stepped immediately into Sheard's shoes.

119

"Any idea what time you'll be coming back tomorrow?"

"Not before afternoon. Petrie will see you're informed."

"One other thing." Vaughan hesitated, knowing the extent to which Howard was gambling. "After last night's blitz and the way the campaign's accelerating . . . what . . . what if this doesn't work?"

"It'll work," Howard said. It had to work.

"Say Leach isn't our man."

"Then he's eliminated and we start all over."

He said it angrily, as though his judgment had suddenly been called into question. He turned away without another word and went to be checked in.

It was Leach, all right. And he was going to get Leach. Eight hundred miles and back, and Leach would wish he'd never been born.

Petrie had been two years in Warsaw and he didn't much care for it, not for the more obvious reasons but simply because there was nowhere to play golf. Not only in Warsaw; there wasn't a course anywhere in the whole country.

He blew his nose and stamped his feet, watching Howard's plane taxi in towards the modest terminal building at Okecie Airport. High, very high, mother-of-pearl cloud streamers were shredding in a silent wind, but at ground level the air was motionless, heavy with cold, dead. Last night's snow was sprinkled everywhere, not much, but enough to remind you of what would soon be coming. Petrie hated this kind of winter: Rome had spoiled him, once and for all.

"Hello," he said, smiling, when Howard finally came through the barrier. "Good trip?"

It was years since they'd met, four at least, yet he remembered Howard's handshake as if from yesterday: like a vice. They exchanged greetings, rapidly looking each other over. Telex messages gave you no idea, but the eyes told everything: you could read between the lines.

120

"The car's outside," Petrie said.

"Okay."

They were much the same build, much the same age. They walked over to the car, and Petrie slid behind the wheel. He limped a bit on the left leg and there were only three fingers on his left hand—legacies from Suez, it was said.

"Lucky break for the P.M. last night. Absolute miracle, from all accounts."

"You're right," Howard agreed. "But for a speaking engagement in Stafford he'd have been in the car—sure as I'm sitting here."

"They haven't made many mistakes, not if the last few days are anything to go by."

"You're right," Howard repeated. They nosed carefully into the traffic's erratic flow. "Where are you taking me now?"

"The Embassy."

They must have covered at least a mile without either of them mentioning anything except the weather, Howard looking to this side and that as the city began to build itself uncertainly around them. But presently, as if he couldn't contain himself any longer, he asked what he wanted most to know.

"Where is he now?"

"At Radom," Petrie answered. "He went there with the Saxon trailer, but he'll be back this evening. It's only about sixty miles."

They sat in Petrie's neat, overheated office in the elegant neo-Renaissance villa on the Avenue Roz and played the latest of the tapes.

"*From Ireland I would go on to England?*"

"*That's right.*"

"*Openly? With a passport?*"

"*That's right. Someone I know in London can help us there.*"

121

"The 'someones' you know ..."

Every word, every sound, no imagination necessary.

Hard-faced, Howard listened, one leg slung across the other, fingers tapping the raised knee. He had no misgivings about listening any more.

"Although we've been able to bug her flat," Petrie said, "it hasn't been possible anywhere else. Leach changes rooms at the hotel each time he comes, and in any case he's not there very much these days. Last month we had a shot at doing something about the trailer, but it didn't work out, and I'm not sure when we'll ever have the sort of opportunity we need. So we've had to rely on what we can get from this Dabrowska place."

"What's the name again?"

"Dabrowska. She's out most of the day and the flat's unattended." Petrie motioned towards the Grundig. "This is evening talk, night talk, morning talk."

"Best times."

"It's paid off, anyway. At last."

"You can say that again."

Petrie went to the window and looked out, interested, it seemed, in something he saw. If Howard was thinking of nailing Leach with what they knew, then London was surely the place for doing it. In Warsaw they were treading on eggshells all the time—and had been for months past.

"What exactly are your plans?" There's been no consultation, the tone inferred. Suddenly you're here and I'm pretty much in the dark as to why. "You don't intend to confront him, do you?"

"That's my intention, yes. Head on."

"When?"

"Tonight."

Petrie turned. Howard seemed to have the bit between his teeth. "Is that wise?"

"Wise or not, it's what I've come for. Inaction now would be a crime."

There was a slight pause, more a hesitation than anything. "We've been playing a pretty delicate game over here for quite a while now, and I don't see—"

"It's what I'll confront him with that'll set the scene."

"Yes?" Petrie said, the inflection irresistible.

"Galatorsko . . . Make or break."

Petrie squinted down at the carpet as if he were sizing up a difficult putt. "You'll blow it doing that. You'll blow the whole shooting match."

"Not if I ask for his help."

"*Leach's?*"

Howard nodded. "Not if I also tell him what he least expects to hear."

"What's that, for God's sake?" Petrie asked.

"Something about Warrick."

It had started snowing again.

"Listen," Howard began, one goal only in his mind. "This is what we're going to do."

Leach reached the Forum from Radom at a quarter to six. He parked the trailer in the usual place and went straight up to Room 448, his eyes smarting after driving through falling snow on roads beginning to crust and freeze. He stripped immediately and ran a bath, lay in it, soaking himself, then toweled and dressed. He had promised Anna he'd be with her by seven, so he was going to manage comfortably and there was no need to call her.

Retman was different, though. Leach went down to the brightness of the foyer and used the pay telephone. "It's imperative for me to see you"—that was the line he would take, firm yet polite. There had been no opportunity earlier in the day. He stood listening to the ringing tone, braced for Retman's quiet "Who's there?" Sweating a little in anticipation, mentally rehearsing a choice of words. So much hung on this. Depending on what he said, and how it was said, things could change.

There was no answer. He tried again, but with the same result. No answer. The hell of it was that he didn't know where Retman lived; the telephone was their only link. He hesitated, ready to leave it, ready to dial once more. He was nowhere near any feeling of dismay, but all the same he was unsettled. Retman had always been there in the past, always, without fail.

In the end he left it. He would call later, from Anna's. That part would be all right. Time and place: he wouldn't mention anything else. But persuading Retman, convincing Retman—that wasn't for the telephone.

Leach hunched deeper into his coat as he went through the outer glass doors into the night. The cold clutched at him instantly and his breath showed like ectoplasm. First thing he must do was garage the trailer.

"Mr. Leach?"

He swung around, a squirm of fear thrusting into his belly. Two men were there, fur-hatted like himself, collars up, hands out of sight. He couldn't imagine where they'd sprung from; no one was about when he stepped outside.

"Mr. Leach?"

"That's correct."

Police?

"Will you come with us, please?"

He could have sworn the voice was English. "What's this in aid of?"

"Please." They crowded him. "We'll talk when we're away from here."

"Who the hell are you?"

124

Some people brushed by with their heads down, oblivious of the drama.

"We're from the Embassy, Mr. Leach. The British Embassy."

"What d'you want?" Leach heard himself, fear in his throat as well. The urge was to bluster, and he somehow fought it off. "I don't understand—"

"Keep moving, Mr. Leach . . . *please.*"

He felt himself propelled by them, one on each side of him. He could have struggled, might have run; but he stayed, panic racing his mind in several different directions simultaneously.

"This way."

Twenty paces or so took them clear of the hotel's entrance. Then Leach stopped, snow falling vertically and crunching underfoot, the look in his eyes as he turned that of somebody at bay.

"Just what the hell's all this about?"

"We want your help, Mr. Leach." The one with the new hat and a facial twitch was doing the talking.

"What kind of help?"

"We'll explain in a minute. *And* we'll also apologize for coming at you like this. But there *are* reasons. Good reasons . . . Now, shall we walk on? The car is over here."

It was a winning style and Leach yielded. The awful panic went out of him; the fear abated. Suspicion and uncertainty and alarm took their place. Everything had been so quick, catching him unawares. He walked to the car, working desperately to steel himself, prepare himself. But for what. *What?* . . . He got into the back, and one of the pair came with him, the other taking the wheel. The doors were slammed to and suddenly the three of them were cocooned together, the windows solid cataract-white.

"I think we first ought to introduce ourselves. . . . My name's Duncan Howard and my colleague's name is Alan Petrie."

125

Leach nodded. It was private here, a place to themselves, unseen traffic sloshing past close by. An orange glow filtered into the car from the overhead street lights and they could see each other vaguely. With great control he said: "What makes two people from the British Embassy behave like gangsters?"

"I'm sorry if we were a bit extreme."

"You could have approached me inside the hotel, surely?"

"We preferred not to risk the public eye."

"Risk?"

"Let's just say we didn't want to be too obvious."

"Why not?" Leach's posture continued cool, with an underlying hint of impatience; somehow he managed it. "What's so special about you and me, may I ask?"

"I'm going to come to that."

Petrie switched on. The starter retched and the engine fired. Leach stiffened, reacting fast.

"What's the idea?"

Petrie fiddled with the heater. "Too damned cold, that's what."

"We're not going anywhere, Mr. Leach," Howard said. "Not for the present, anyway . . . Smoke?"

He watched Leach light up, cupping his hands around the proffered stem of flame. He knew the voice from the tapes and the face from the photograph, yet both seemed only approximations of the real thing. It was a more rounded voice than he'd supposed, better educated, and the structure of the face was weaker than the grainy, blown-up print had revealed.

"What's this about helping you?" Leach said uncertainly. "Why me?"

"Because you'll do it better than anyone else."

"Oh, yes?"

"I promise you."

A nervous snort of a laugh. "You must be joking."

"Far from it."

"Tell me how."

Howard reached into an inner pocket. "I'd like you to look at this, Mr. Leach. . . . Give us a bit of light, Alan."

The ceiling light clicked on. Howard produced a stiff brown envelope and extracted the photograph. It was upside down, and he turned it around.

"This," he said again and passed it across.

Not a muscle moved in Leach's face. Seconds elapsed, Howard watching him sidelong, both of them watching, Petrie, too, but he gave nothing away. Not a flicker. Perhaps the cigarette trembled between his lips, but that was all. It was a remarkable performance. All hell must have been going on inside.

With a show of amused astonishment, he said: "Where'd you get this?" Then: "It's me, isn't it? Me."

"That's right."

"At Galatorsko?"

"Right again."

"Where'd you get it?" He met Howard's gaze and held it somehow, a slight curl on his lips. They might have been turning the pages of an album. "Last year at Galatorsko. That's me by the pool."

Howard said: "It came our way—let's put it like that."

"A business contact invited me over there last summer. I was traveling up from Lublin and I stayed at the place overnight."

"Oh, yes?" Howard used the ensuing silence like a weapon, breaking it when he chose and not before. "Is this contact of yours in the photograph?"

"No." Leach peered. "No." Smoke dribbled from his mouth. He gave the nervous snort again. "I . . . I'm not too sure where this is leading."

"I'll explain," Howard said. He gestured graphically. "Getting our hands on this particular photograph happens to be a quite remarkable bit of luck. . . . Good luck," he

127

added disarmingly. "Not the kind that comes along every day of the week. An outright fluke, if you like."

"How d'you mean?"

"The person you're standing with happens to be someone by the name of Warrick. David Warrick."

Not a flicker. "So?" Leach must have felt trapped. Sweat beaded his forehead, but he still kept his panic battened down. "The name doesn't ring a bell."

"He didn't introduce himself?"

"He may have done, but I don't remember."

Howard's mouth dragged. "You talked with him, though?"

"For a few minutes."

"What about?"

"Odds and ends." Leach shrugged. "It was quite a while ago. I don't recall anything special."

"It didn't surprise you to meet a fellow countryman in such a comparatively remote place?"

A tramcar was grinding by. "Until you mentioned his name just now I didn't realize he *was* British. I meet a helluva lot of people in a helluva lot of different situations and quite a percentage of them have no trace of an accent. I certainly had no idea—"

"Warrick," Howard said, "is a defector."

"Oh?"

"A defector."

"I didn't know that."

Leach took refuge in disposing of his cigarette, winding a window down and flipping the butt away. Howard's eyes never strayed. There were people dead because of him, scores of them. Plus Chisholm and Sheard, wounds in Howard's flesh.

"How was I to know?"

"Once a defector doesn't mean always a defector."

Leach's lips were parted a little. He frowned, fingers on

the go, the one part of him over which he seemed to have no control.

"Not in Warrick's book, anyway," Howard said, and let the silence hang.

"You've lost me, I'm afraid. . . . I don't understand."

"We have reason to believe that Warrick's tired of it over there."

It fell like a stone.

"He wants to come out, Mr. Leach."

This time there was a crack in Leach's self-control. For a long-drawn second terror showed in his eyes. His mouth went out of shape and he seemed to freeze, abolutely rigid. Then the instant passed and the terror changed into fear, alarm, dismay—degrees he could almost master. Almost, but not quite. In the back seat of the car Howard could feel him tremble.

"How do you know this?"

"He's started making soundings. . . . Recently."

"But who would he—?"

Leach cut himself off. God oh God oh God. He wiped the sweat from his face, on a knife edge, panic building up again. "What exactly are you trying to put together?" His voice wavered. "You said something about a fluke. An outright fluke, that's what you said."

"The fluke," Howard said carefully, "is having this evidence of Warrick and you being at Galatorsko. It's something I believe we can employ to our advantage."

" 'We'?"

"That's right."

Leach moistened his lips, but said nothing, mind on the rampage.

"You see, Mr. Leach, the truth of the matter is that Warrick isn't wanted back in England. He'd be too much of an embarrassment in too many quarters." Howard's tone was confidential. "No doubt he hopes to do some kind of deal. What he's sure to try to offer are names of contacts and associates in exchange for an amnesty for himself.... D'you follow me?"

Leach jerked a nod.

"Well, there'll be no deal. For reasons I'm not in a position to enlarge on, he wouldn't be welcomed back home. ... Let's say it'd be better if he didn't return."

Leach frowned, confused, his mouth dry and his heart thudding.

"What's the photograph got to do with all this?"

"It'll help put the stamp of truth on what we'd like you to do for us."

Petrie took over, craning around. "There's a man in London—a journalist—who specializes in this kind of story. What we're asking is for you to feed it to him."

"Couldn't anyone do that?"

"He wouldn't touch it if he thought it was a plant."

Leach delayed, hesitating, still in the grip of shock. "Who is he?"

"Steven Dekker. A scoop merchant. Dangle an exclusive in front of him and he'll bite—so long as he's convinced it's genuine." Petrie nodded at the photograph, which had remained on Howard's lap. "That'll convince him. Show him that, and he'll listen."

"And what exactly would I tell him?"

"That Warrick's asked you to sound out his chances of repatriation."

"I was at Galatorsko months ago."

"What of it?" Howard said quickly. "The picture at least proves that you and Warrick met. The approach about repatriation can have happened since. Here," he suggested, smoothing Leach into the con. "Here in Warsaw—during the past few days, say. Why not?"

Someone rapped on the windshield. Petrie opened his window with a start, framing the pinched face of a militiaman. A brief exchange took place between them, the muzzle of the militiaman's automatic carbine poking above the battoned-down cap into the smear of lights beyond.

"*Naturalnie*," Petrie said eventually. "*Dobrze: dobrze.*" He smiled at the man by way of farewell and sealed the three of them in again. "Fellow doesn't like where we're parked."

"That's all?"—Howard.

"Thanks to C.D. exemption." Petrie started the wipers laboring and dropped solidly into gear. He pulled out from the curb and headed down Marszalkowska, the ceiling light off, their heads and shoulders in silhouette. "Round and round—okay, Duncan?"

"Okay," Howard said. They went a little way, the snow as heavy as on a Christmas card. "You're a very elusive man, Mr. Leach."

"I am?" Leach felt sick, scared in more ways then he'd yet grasped.

"You took some tracking down, believe me. Once we'd decided on a course of action about Warrick, you've been conspicuous by your absence from the Forum."

"I travel a lot."

"Yes."

"Today I was at Radom."

"That's right."

We know, it sounded like. We know a great deal. Who you are, where you go, what you do. Who you meet . . . Leach swallowed drily, panic never quite absent. Retman a part of it, Anna as well. He'd been on his way to Anna when this started.

"Warrick's only put feelers out during the past few days. We've had to move a bit. Cut corners—know what I mean?"

At the very center of his fears Leach remained stunned. If Warrick started trading names, he was done for. Disaster was suddenly as close as that. He struggled to discipline his mind and lit a cigarette, clumsy doing it, the glow like a firefly in the dark.

With skill and timing Howard said: "You'll be doing your country a service, Mr. Leach."

Words, words. "What's the journalist's name again?"

"Dekker."

"I . . . I won't be back in London until Friday week."

"We can't wait that long," Howard said. "What I'd like to suggest is that you contact him tomorrow."

"*Tomorrow?*" Leach turned his head and stared.

"I'd like to suggest that you fly to Heathrow tomorrow morning and fly back to Warsaw in the evening."

The cigarette glowed, sufficient for Petrie to glimpse Howard's tinted face in the rearview mirror. Stone hard, the eyes quite merciless. Yet the voice was friendly, that of a colleague, an appreciative ally.

"Don't you do it ever?" Howard was saying. "There and back the same day?"

"I have."

"It's a very special favor we're asking of you. Very special. But we attach such importance to the news about Warrick being leaked in the most plausible way possible that I'm absolutely certain we can rely on your willing co-operation."

Everything was going too quickly for Leach. But he couldn't refuse, daren't refuse. That much he already knew. He must do as Howard wanted. *Must.* The irony was inescapable, but he was beyond any appreciation of irony. All he was aware of was that he had no option but to be in London fast.

Others had to be told. Besides Dekker.

"Will you help us, Mr. Leach?"

"Yes," he said.

Retman for a start, Retman first of all.

"It goes without saying that you'll be put to no personal expense. By this time tomorrow evening—if you so wish—you'll be back in Warsaw."

132

"I understand."

"There'll be no problem with your employers?"

"No."

"Or your work schedule?"

"No."

"Are you quite sure?" Howard laid it on a bit. "If you felt it was essential, I could put the matter to Sir Gordon Saxon, though—naturally—I'd much rather not."

"It won't be necessary," Leach said.

The danger wasn't here in the car any more. The focal point had shifted suddenly. Now it was on Warrick and what Warrick might do and say. The first temptation was always betrayal.

With what he thought was cunning, Leach said: "Does anyone know where Warrick is right now?"

"Yesterday," Petrie answered willingly, "he was reported in Lisbon."

They knew so much, these two. Lisbon made a likely steppingstone. Leach leaned back, nerves hard held, an unnatural sweat stinging his neck. He shivered involuntarily, ice and fire. In Nowy Swiat there were glittering shop-window displays to catch the eye, but he was blind to them. They went on past the snow-heaped statue of Copernicus and the brightness of the Bristol Hotel, down into the reconstructed miracle of the Old Town, places where he'd walked with Anna, none of which he saw now.

A doubt seemed to heave his mind. "Tell me how releasing this information via Dekker is going to warn Warrick off."

"It won't," Howard said.

"No?"

"I daresay he'll continue to make overtures, leak or no leak."

"Then what's the purpose of all this?"

Howard took his time. They were zigzagging down to the Vistula. "I can't divulge everything, Mr. Leach. I'm sure

133

you appreciate that. But, in fairness, this much I believe I *can* say."

"Yes?"

"When Dekker let's his story loose there'll be someone who we hope will break under the news. Someone highly placed, someone who goes back to the time of Warrick's defection, someone who—up to now—we haven't been able to touch."

So that was it.

Leach's relief was fleeting. Past and present were all one, and Warrick straddled both. God knows how many throats he could cut.

"I told you," Howard went on, "we don't want Warrick back, not at any price. But with the authority of a Steven Dekker exclusive we can maybe have the best of both worlds. . . . It's a gamble, of course, the whole damn thing's a gamble." The lights in the apartment blocks to their right pricked rectangular patterns in the swirling snow. "For my part, Mr. Leach, I'm extremely grateful to you for your willingness to assist, and for being so forgiving about the unorthodoxy of our approach. But chance saw to it that Galatorsko has given you a vital part to play and—well, we thought it advisable in the circumstances not to contact you in a more normal manner. And, for the same reason, when we finally separate, we'll do so some distance from the Forum—yes?"

They were another half hour together, all of that, on the move throughout—Old Town, New Town, as far as the outlying suburbs in one direction, across the river in another. And while Petrie drove, Howard gave Leach a thorough briefing, rehearsed him, perfected him in what was to be said and the attitude he should adopt; that, Howard explained, was as important as anything else. There were air tickets, too, plus Dekker's address and telephone number, all neatly together in a folder which Howard handed over.

134

"You see, Mr. Leach, how sure we were you wouldn't let us down."

Leach left them two whole blocks from the Forum, the car never quite coming to a standstill. Seconds after the door was slammed shut and they started to accelerate away the snow had obliterated him.

"Well?"

"Hooked," Petrie said.

"Think so?"

"Absolutely."

"Bluff, double bluff. Catch-as-catch-can." The side of Howard's mouth went, strain plucking at the muscle, and the taut cheek quivered as though it had been stung. Everything he felt was written on his face in lines and shadows. Leach had taught him what it was to hate and it showed now, etched into his tiredness.

"Tomorrow will tell."

"He'll go, all right," Petrie said, braking for a red light. "He'll be on the plane."

"Oh, yes, he'll go." No doubts on that score. "It's who he warns when he gets there—that's what'll count. Whether we can spot it."

"I thought you played it beautifully. Really led him by the nose."

"We'll see." Howard had no time for praise. "We'll have to wait and see."

The light changed to green as they slowed, releasing them along with a gaggle of other cars. They headed back to the Embassy, dark slushy tracks where the traffic spattered along.

"What d'you bet he's on the telephone already?"

"Wouldn't you be doing that if you were in his shoes?" Howard felt drained, the headache back again. "Taking his local contact out of circulation was an essential precaution. . . . Neat."

135

"More bruises than anything, the driver reported. Perhaps a broken leg. The ambulance went to the hospital in the Mirow district."

"D'you have his name?"

"Not yet." Petrie shook his head. "All we know for sure is that he's the selfsame person Leach meets at the Chopin Monument in Lazienki Park each time he comes to Warsaw." He produced an ivory grin of satisfaction. So much had happened in this one day alone. "The driver swears it looked more like a genuine accident than the real thing."

22

Twice Leach dialed the Retman number and got no answer, restlessly shifting his weight from foot to foot, phoning from the downstairs lobby of the Forum.

Retman could nip Warrick in the bud.

B-rrrlll . . . B-rrrlll . . .

Alarm was clenched around Leach's heart as he cut off and tried again.

B-rrrlll . . . B-rrrlll . . . B-rrrlll . . .

The thin ringing tone seemed to mock him. For the best part of an hour he'd sat and suffered, cooped up with Howard and Petrie with his nerves swinging like a pendulum from initial terror to a false sense of relief and through everything in between.

Come on, he urged. Come *on*.

Still no answer. He hung up and wrenched himself away. A patrolling tart with vivid eyes and dyed red hair spoke to him softly as he shouldered by, but he didn't really hear or see. He went out into the night again and drove the big Saxon mobile unit over to the place where he kept it garaged. From there he walked to Anna's; little likelihood of a taxi with the weather the way it was. He walked fast, since it was eight already, prodded by a sense of urgency.

And frightened, more frightened now than when he was in the car.

Where in the hell was Retman?

Time and again he had come to Anna needing to be loved, to be awakened as only she knew how. But he had never imagined he would come to her as he was coming now, in weakness and in fear. He was desperately vulnerable. All at once he seemed to be losing both his nerve and the ability to stay calm. And he felt so exposed, so alone.

Who took the picture at Galatorsko? And had there been others since? Where, if so, and with whom?

He fretted as he walked, question marks galore, things he hadn't risked asking. Chance, was it? It had to be, *had to be*. Nothing made sense otherwise, but Christ he was close to the wind. The irony stared him in the face again and this time he acknowledged it. Chance was a freak, but it had him by the throat now.

Warrick must be stopped; silenced. Somehow. Here or in London.

He stamped and shook the snow from himself and went up the gloomy stairs to Anna's flat two at a time. His thumb had scarcely left the bellpush when she opened the door, relieved to see him, a small anxious frown still there with her greeting.

"You're so late."

"I got held up. I was out at Radom, and—"

"I thought something must have happened." She took his coat. "Something bad . . . But no, thank God."

It was so warm here. Leach held her close, kissing her.

"I needed that," she said. "Now everything is all right again."

He poured a measure from the vodka bottle, knocked it back and felt the spreading glow. Twice he filled the glass to the brim.

"Come and eat," Anna said, cupping his face in her hands as she passed. How she longed, her green eyes said, to see the tension go out of him. "You are so tired."

"I have to telephone."

"Can't it wait?"

"No," he said, sharper than he realized.

He crossed the room and dialed Retman. And even as the familiar tone started ringing against his ear again he knew, with lead in his heart, that no one was going to answer. He slammed the receiver down. Retman was his only link; from the first it had been so. There was nobody else to contact, nobody else to inform that Warrick was about to renege. He went back to the bottle a third time, scared ever since they'd walked him to the car outside the Forum.

"What are you afraid of?" Anna asked, quick to read the torment in him. They were at the table in the alcove by the window. "Tell me what you are afraid of."

There was love in her voice. He had never imagined he would need or earn this kind of love.

"Is it about us?"

First he shook his head, but then he nodded and said: "Yes." He didn't know what was happening to him.

"Yes or no?"

"Yes."

"The phone call?"

"Not exactly."

She stopped eating. Her eyes searched into his. "What is the truth, Martin? It's hopeless, isn't it? Hopeless for you and me."

"No," he said without conviction, dragging his mind to where she wanted it. "No, it's not hopeless."

"Will we go next month?"

"I can't answer that."

"Ever?"

He couldn't speak. She began to weep and he couldn't speak, silent tears in her eyes. All he could do was look elsewhere. He had trained himself to steer swiftly away from any memory that threatened him, taught himself to cope alone, learned from life never to confide. But now everything was conspiring at once and he didn't know where he was or how to manage. He locked his hands and felt sweat prick his forehead. And Retman's words rose up to taunt him: "Take care. You could drown yourself in that."

"Don't cry, Anna."

Now it was she who looked away.

"Please," Leach said. "It's not what you think."

He waited, frightened and out of his depth, needing her trust and support as never before.

"I'm in a mess, Anna."

"Because of me?"

He saw a flicker of alarm, and said "No" instantly. "But it affects us."

She dried her tears with the backs of her hands. "Tell me."

Again he found difficulty in speaking, like a dislocation between brain and tongue. "I need your help."

"How?"

"There's something I must tell you."

"Go on."

"Last year I was in Galatorsko—around midsummer. I . . . I met a man there who asked me if I would agree to be a carrier for him."

"Carrier?"

"Smuggler."

She sucked in air. "Oh, *no!*"

Leach nodded.

"And you did?"

139

"I did, yes." Now it was coming. "I still do."

"Oh my God," she said. "Oh my God, Martin—why? Why?"

"For money."

"Who is the man?"

He launched into an explanation but she interrupted.

"An Englishman?"

"Yes," he said bitterly.

She was bewildered. "But how can an Englishman—?"

He told her. Their voices cut into one another's, staccato question and answer, sometimes a brief dawning silence. For Leach it was like a letting of blood. A longing swept him to be free of Warrick and Retman, to bury the past and escape the present, to go with Anna and begin again.

"How much are you paid?"

"A thousand pounds. Each time a thousand pounds."

"And what do you carry?"

"Radio equipment." His eyes shied away. He would lie to the last. Some things she must never know.

"And you take this radio equipment from Poland?"

"Leipzig," he corrected. "Not from Poland. Poland has nothing to do with it."

"In the trailer?"

"That's right."

"To Ireland?"

"Transshipped out of Rotterdam."

Anna had lit a cigarette: he had never known her to do this before. She inhaled nervously, and went on gazing at him through the smoke.

"I undertook to carry ten consignments. What I've been trying to do is to persuade them to release me from making a delivery next month. . . . So that there would be room for you."

"And they said no?"

"They said no. Warrick pulls the strings on me from here."

140

Her lower lip quivered. "God, what a mess."

"That's . . . that's why I told you we'd maybe have to wait until next summer." He paused, needing her, dreading that she might despise him. "Do you understand now?"

She nodded. "You shouldn't have kept me from the truth."

"It was something that started before we met, and I—"

"Loving means trusting." Her distress was very near the surface. She reached for his hands across the table. The food was going cold on their plates. "Martin," she said, dismay and reproach and anxiety all there. "How can we build a life together if this is how we begin? *To niedobrze.*"

"I've been a fool," he muttered.

"How big is the risk you take each time?"

Leach gave a small shrug. "I know how to get by."

"You have to go on with it? Every month?"

"Until May."

"What if you change your mind? . . . Refuse?"

"I'm not in a position to do that."

"You could return the money." She was unaware of why such a price was paid, just as he had closed his mind to it.

"No." He thought of the caress of Retman's voice, the soft threat in the back of the throat. "If I don't keep my side of the bargain, they'll break me, Anna. Finish me."

He drank with a tossing jerk of the head. He was sweating now again and he searched the curling smoke for the concern in her eyes.

"There's something else."

"How do you mean?"

"I've been approached by people from the British Embassy."

"When?"

"This evening. That's why I was late."

" 'Approached'?"

"About Warrick." Leach nodded. "The Englishman Warrick."

She screwed the butt in a saucer. With the air of some-one who felt she couldn't grasp too much more she said: "What about Warrick?"

He explained. And grew frightened as he explained, scared all over again. Somehow he'd got to thread his way clear, escape.

"I'm in the middle, Anna. . . . All because of a photo-graph, one bloody fluke photograph."

She took a long time, her tears mastered, her gaze un-flinching, all the control there he so badly needed.

"You should count your good-luck stars." She must have lifted it from a phrase book. "Isn't it better that you know? Isn't it better to have been told what is happening? To have been asked to take part in what these people are doing?"

He was lost. She saw it now. Lost and desperate. He got up from the table and paced back and forth.

"You won't make the room bigger, doing that."

He swung around. "What Howard wants me for isn't to do with me—that's the hell of it, that's the crazy part. He's got someone else in mind, somebody already under surveillance. But what I'm expected to do won't put a gag in Warrick's mouth. Warrick'll talk if he gets the chance. He'll name me if it suits him."

"You seem so sure."

"It stands to reason," he flared. "That's why I have to contact Retman. He's my best bet. Once Retman's been informed, then Warrick can be tackled from *this* side, before any damage is done."

"But isn't Warrick in Lisbon?"

"That's right."

The feeling of panic rose again, slow but insistent, like a bubble trapped in oil. Nine steps took Leach to the phone. He snatched the thing off its rest, dialed, waited, waited and waited. Anna came over and joined him, head tilted a little, close enough to hear what he heard.

B-rrrlll . . . B-rrrlll . . .

She said: "It's early yet."

"I've tried all evening."

"Even so."

He hung up, jaws clenched, eyes glinting. Time was using itself up and the awful feeling was that others were employing it—Howard and Petrie and Warrick, each of them in danger of exposing the truth of his own position with every passing hour. He turned away and stared out the window, seeing the snow still powdering down and the lights of the cars crossing the long smooth sweep of the Poniatowski bridge, the desire to escape never stronger, moved to a sudden and crushing envy for the safety of other people's lives.

There was so much to survive.

"You will have to go to London," Anna was telling him. "You haven't really any choice."

It registered vaguely.

"Whether or not you get in touch with this person here, you will have to go."

"Yes."

"You must do as they say. It's important not to give them the slightest reason to be angry with you."

"Yes."

"And then, when this is all over, you must forget it ever happened. You and I must get away, start afresh. One more tightrope, you and me together, but nothing more . . . Ever."

"Yes," he said.

She knew, she explained. She *knew* that everything would be all right. Everybody made mistakes, did stupid things, got caught up in situations they didn't really understand. He listened, hanging on every word despite her only knowing half the story, touched by what he must mean to her for her to counsel with such care and concern.

"Warrick won't damage you, Martin."

143

He put out a hand and gently squeezed the back of her neck, seeing the green eyes soften. "I wish I had your confidence."

"Don't worry so. They don't want him over there in England, you told me. So how will his telling them your name make them change their mind? I ask you. . . . What have you done but smuggle some radio equipment? If there are names to be named, it is the big ones they will bite on. Not yours, darling, not yours."

He listened. He loved her and needed her; not only now but always. Four times more he called Retman, but each time it was in vain. "Wait till morning," Anna calmed him. "Try again then." He listened; such strength in her voice, such certainty. "No matter what, be sure to take the plane tomorrow. Do exactly what they want. You're on their side, don't you see? You've everything to gain by keeping it that way."

They went to bed. He listened, tense and tired and restless, holding her, sometimes with her lips brushing his.

"Martin . . ."

"Yes?"

"Come back tomorrow night. Don't stay over there."

She slept eventually, slipping away. But sleep was impossible for him. He lay unblinking on his side while fear chased in and out of his mind and the throbbing beat of his heart sounded endlessly against the pillow, like a drummer in the dark.

23

The very last thing Howard had done before Leach got out of the car was to hand him the photograph. And the very last thing he'd stressed was that they should travel separately.

"Don't acknowledge me. And sit well away on the plane."

"I didn't realize you'd be on the same flight."

"Oh, yes," Howard said. "But until we're cleared at Heathrow it'd be better if we didn't know one another. You're clean over here," he threw in as a disarming postscript, "whereas I'm not so sure about myself."

Now, in bitter cold, Leach walked with a straggle of other people to the waiting Polish Air Lines Ilyushin. Sometime during the night the snow had stopped falling and it lay everywhere pure and smooth except on the cleared runways and approach lanes, the air shifting erratically, the sky leaden, the clouds low.

"Good morning." A stewardess's trained smile at the top of the gangway. "*Dzien dobry.*"

Leach chose a seat on the port side, four rows back. Howard had been in the spartan departure lounge along with the rest of the passengers and he was one of the last to climb aboard, yawning as he did so. His eyes flicked over Leach in exactly the same fashion as they flicked over everybody else—no interest, not enough sleep, just wanting a place to sit and doze the flight away, that was all.

He moved crab-wise out of Leach's view, along the tube of the fuselage. Leach touched his pockets as he belted himself in. He had brought no baggage; everything he carried was in his pockets—wallet, passport, return-flight ticket, photograph—and he checked to feel that they were with him.

For the nth time.

The engines were switched on and the plane shivered

145

gently. The noise increased, drowning the hiss of the air conditioning. They went at a crawl out to the turning circle and the roar rose and fell as if a door kept being opened and shut.

No Retman. Nine-twelve and about to fly, the last chance of speaking to Retman gone to waste forty minutes ago.

B-rrrlll . . . *B-rrrlll* . . . In the departure lounge. *B-rrrlll* . . . *B-rrrlll.*

Leach had given up, sick of the sound, his unease sustained. Chance knew how to cheat, all right. It was Retman's function to be there to provide the link, and up to now he'd never failed. Not once.

The plane made its run and lifted off. They climbed into the overcast above a serene all-white world, and Warsaw's outer suburbs tilted sharply as they began to fade from view. Leach lit a cigarette and pressed back into his seat, no one beside him, alone with his thoughts. Today was a day of obligation in more ways than one.

Retman wasn't the only link in the chain. Gray must learn about Warrick, too; Gray at Golden Jacey's.

Warrick, Retman, Leach, Gray, Nolan—the chain was as strong as its constituent parts. No less, no more. And as safe. Nolan in Ireland, Gray in London, Retman in Warsaw. Warrick had spelled it out at Galatorsko, standing by the pool that day, a squat square-faced ex-sergeant with rimless tinted glasses and the good clothes of a much traveled man.

"Fifty boxes a month, Mr. Leach. Five hundred in all. What d'you say? Provide my friends with the muscle they need and earn yourself ten thousand pounds . . . ?"

Leach exhaled, eyes closed, vividly remembering the rose beds banked at the sides of the pool and the sunlight jazzing on the jade-green water and the sound of laughter as children played, chasing one another.

He hadn't asked what "muscle" meant: hadn't wanted to, hadn't dared. Ten thousand pounds had brought the shutters down, made him dumb, made him blind—there and then and ever since.

Until Anna. Until now.

Retman in Warsaw, Gray in London, Nolan in Ireland . . .

And now Warrick was suddenly in Lisbon with a turntail wish in his heart and names to offer by way of makeweight—names and routes and sources and every damn thing.

Again Leach felt a cold stream of alarm flush swiftly through his guts. Gray had to know—and through Gray, Nolan. Golden Jacey's opened up at noon, and as soon as possible afterwards that was where he must go.

Dekker first. Feed Dekker with the Howard story, produce the picture, be convincing, "at all costs be convincing"—Howard. They'd be down before one. . . . Finish with Dekker first of all. Then contact Gray. Then double back to Warsaw and get hold of Retman. Right away, before it was too late.

"Come back tomorrow night," Anna had murmured. "Don't stay over there."

Not if he could help it. There was more to be done than sow the seeds of his own salvation. He was lost without her, weak and out of his depth, always panicky. And he so wanted to live. To live. Really to live and have done with it all.

The next time Leach saw land there was no snow. Green fields, gravel pits, patterns of houses and light industry, an oblique glimpse of Windsor Castle away in the distance—but nowhere any snow. The Ilyushin bucked heavily as it headed in, and Leach thought they had used up a lot of the runway before the wheels made jarring contact and the reverse-thrust din rose to a fierce shuddering crescendo. Otherwise the flight was perfect. And just as well: he had rattled nerves enough as it was.

"Good-bye, sir. Fly LOT again next time. . . . *Do widzenia.*"

A watery sun was halfway up in the sky, and the mildness of the air surprised him. Leach bussed back to the terminal building, strap-hanging within a few feet of Howard, the one glance they chanced to exchange that of total strangers. They stood separately in line at Immigration, but Leach was through Customs while everyone else was still waiting for their baggage to come up.

Nothing to declare . . . He walked out like a free man and chose a place where he could stand and discreetly catch Howard's eye when he, too, emerged. Nearby, a uniformed chauffeur was reading the *Mail* and the headlines were inches deep.

QUEEN'S VISIT TO COMMONWEALTH INSTITUTE
UNPRECEDENTED SECURITY MEASURES

He was there for a good five minutes before Howard came through the doors and went briskly past. He followed, a dozen paces to the rear, obeying his instructions to the letter. Not until they shared the garage lift did they join forces, no one else with them as they sealed themselves in.

"Mild, isn't it?" was all Howard said. "Incredible."

He seemed edgy, as if he hadn't cared for the pretense. He took the Granada smoothly down the ramp and through the labyrinth of Heathrow's traffic lanes and out onto the eastbound highway, heading for London and driving fast.

"Any questions? Second thoughts?"

"No," Leach said.

"Where'll I drop you off?"

"Brook Green. I'll make the call to Dekker from my flat."

BOMBINGS: C.I.V.A. ADMITS TOUCHBUTTON RESPONSIBILITY

The placards directed themselves at Leach, reminders of everything he didn't want to know. Boxes, Warrick had talked of, not blood in the streets, nothing quite real then, not even the money, the sharp end of the truth of it all a long way from Warsaw and Leipzig and Rotterdam.

"Don't overplay it with Dekker."

"I'll try not to."

"The worst thing that could happen now is for the whole business to stall. So—whatever you do—don't make out you're all that hard to get."

"I won't."

"My bet is that if you offer Dekker an inch he'll want a yard. That's what I'm banking on."

They didn't do much talking. Everything was agreed between them, settled. Leach smoked a lot, but many people did that, no giveaway there. The traffic was patchy and they were half an hour together before reaching Hammersmith; from there Brook Green was only a stone's throw.

Howard asked: "You'll return to Warsaw tonight?"

"If possible."

He pulled in and braked by the curb. "I won't say more, Mr. Leach, except to repeat my gratitude. It's an extraordinary use we're making of you, extraordinary but vital, as I'm sure you understand."

He offered a hand and Leach took it, managing to hold the gaze as well, running with the hare and hunting with the hounds.

"Bye, then. And thank you again."

"Bye." Leach nodded, unclipping his belt.

"Contact Petrie at the Embassy when you get back about your expenses."

"I'll do that."

Leach got out and walked away. And the corner of Howard's mouth gave a convulsive jerk as he watched him go.

Amateur, he thought. Butcher.

Now it was Dekker's turn.

≋ 24

The almost overwhelming temptation was to make for Golden Jacey's there and then: it was after two o'clock and Gray would be doing one of his stints. Even as Leach walked from the car the urge was there, a fluttering renewal of panic about being at Warrick's mercy and time running out. But he managed to put it down.

Dekker first. Then Gray . . . An effort was needed. He had to steel his mind and force himself to deal with Dekker without delay, more than one reason for doing so, the most potent being that he couldn't entirely believe Howard had casually let him loose. So much was at stake for Howard as well, and men like him took nothing on trust. Already, as he turned into the quietness of Brook Green, Leach was aware of a kind of pressure on the back of his neck, inconclusive yet telltale, like the weight of another person's scrutiny, the same sensation as when Retman sometimes came up from behind at their meetings in Warsaw.

Imagination or not, he was taking no chances. Dekker, then Gray . . . Then Retman.

His flat was on the first floor. Two weeks' mail was waiting for him scattered inside the door. Bills and circulars, mainly; not many people ever wrote. He gathered it up and moved carefully from room to room, alert to any changes, nostrils flared to the lifeless air. In September, when he'd arrived home, he could have sworn things weren't quite where they should have been—a vase on a window ledge, shirts in a drawer, even cans in the kitchen cupboard. Galatorsko had given him an extra sense, but—right or wrong that time—there was nothing incriminating in the flat, and never had been. Word of mouth could put an end to him; nothing else.

He went into the kitchen and ran the cold tap and freshened out his mouth. It was strange to be home; he felt he didn't properly belong there. Anna was home now. He got Dekker's number from the folder Howard had given him, lit a cigarette, and dialed.

"Mr. Dekker? ... Mr. Steven Dekker?"

"Speaking, yes."

"I've got a story, Mr. Dekker." Saying what he'd been told to say. "Right out of this world."

"Who are you?"

"I'd like to come and talk with you, Mr. Dekker."

"Who are you?" Not the sort of voice he'd expected: bright, friendly.

"My name's Leach," he said. "Martin Leach."

"And what's this story all about?"

"Someone who's changed his mind."

"People do that every day."

"Not this person."

"Who're we talking about?"

"I'd rather not say on an open line. But I'll tell you this, Mr. Dekker. This story's right up your street."

Crackling raced irritably along the line.

"Why come to me?"

"I know the kind of thing you handle, Mr. Dekker."

"Tell me who the person is."

"Not now."

"Tell me now, or hang up." A bite there suddenly. "I've got other things to do."

"Warrick," Leach said, snatching.

"Come again?"

"Warrick ... David Warrick."

"Oh, yes?" A very slight pause, but absolute surprise, the surprise somehow conveyed. Then Dekker said: "All right, then ... Yes, well, I'd better tell you where I am."

———

Howard reached Buckingham Gate at twenty past two. Someone had taken Sheard's name off the door, he noticed. And there was a memo on his desk saying that Jenny Knight would be back at work in the morning.

"How'd it go, sir?" This was Vaughan, following Howard in before he'd so much as hung his coat.

"Okay so far."

"He's here, then?"

Howard nodded. "With a tail on him. From now on we can only keep our fingers crossed."

"I'll bring you File Nine," Vaughan said. "There's a Telex in from Warsaw."

The Telex read: *On overnight tapes retrieved from apartment subject mentions association with W and admits to role of carrier for ten monthly deliveries on his behalf. Subject extremely jumpy owing to intention of W and absence of his own local contact here. Indications for London therefore more than promising. Tallyho. Petrie.*

Howard read it through twice, then turned the page, excitement savage through his weariness, flipping back to the Special Branch breakdown of Leach's known points of call during the previous four months—*Odeon Cinema, Kensington High Street; Albert Hall; Blue Angel Restaurant, King's Road; Golden Jacey's, St. Martin's Lane; The Grapes, Hammersmith; Green Lane, Bromley.*

"I want these places watched, every entrance, every exit, round the clock. Intensive observation, inside and out, starting right away. Fix it, will you—as of now. This is over and above the existing tail."

"Yes, sir."

"And I want to be informed the moment Leach shows. Wherever and whenever."

"Yes, sir."

Howard pushed the file away. His head was throbbing. It had come to this, then. After all the guesswork and the gambling they were getting close at last.

152

"Mr. Leach?" Dekker's smile was all mouth, the eyes as shrewd as hell.

"That's right."

"Come in, come in."

It was a welcome of sorts. He led Leach through to his sitting room. Putney bridge was visible through the windows, and the silver train sliding past on the elevated track belonged to the District Line.

"No trouble finding me, I hope?"

"I left that to the taxi driver."

"Ah, yes. Of course." Dekker stroked his freckled bird's-egg scalp with one hand and indicated a chair with the other. "Well now, let's come to the point, shall we? What's this about Warrick?"

Leach began with Howard's suggested lead: "Before we go into that I'd like to know what this'll be worth."

"To you or to me?"

"To me."

"I do a standard deal. The split's seventy-five twenty-five, no matter who you are. In my favor. A legal contract, and no bull. Always provided the story's genuine, worth my while, and hasn't been hawked round for a month of Sundays."

"This one hasn't."

"Okay." Dekker's creased neck was like perished brown rubber. "But you'll have to prove it. How in the blazes do you know anything about Warrick, for instance?"

"I've met him."

"Where?"

"Poland."

"What d'you do, for God's sake, that takes you to somewhere like Poland?"

Leach explained.

"When did you meet him?"

"At a place called Galatorsko."

"When, I said, not where."

"During the summer."

Leach felt into his breast pocket and fished out the photograph. He passed it across, and Dekker squinted at it shortsightedly.

"You on the left and Warrick on the right?"

"Correct."

Dekker said the very thing Leach expected, both following Howard's guidelines, both playing it the way they'd been instructed. "Was this the only time you met him?"

"No."

"When was the last time?"

"Eight days ago," Leach lied.

Dekker raised an eyebrow, impressed, no doubt about it. "Same place?"

"Warsaw."

"By chance? Or by design?"

"He asked to see me, if that's what you mean. Not the other way round."

"About what?"

"Coming home," Leach said.

Dekker whistled softly. He limped across the room to an upright piano and reached for a cigarette box.

"Why'd he pick on you?"

"I've no idea."

"He's a pretty hot property—you know that, I suppose?"

Leach nodded.

"How did you find him? . . . Disillusioned?"

"Very much so. I think, the second time, he wanted to sound me out about his chances. He's very out of touch."

"And how did you advise him?"

"I didn't."

"Cigarette?"

They lit up and the smoke swirled. By four, Leach told himself, he must be at Golden Jacey's. Four, at the latest.

"All this is very interesting," Dekker said. "Very interesting indeed."

"I'm glad you find it so."

"There's only one thing wrong with it as far as I'm concerned."

"Yes?"

"It's out of date."

Leach misunderstood. "This photograph merely proves that Warrick and I actually met. Last summer's last summer, I agree. But we've been in contact much more recently than that."

"And I believe you," Dekker said. "But the fact is that this story of yours has been overtaken by events."

A thud of the heart this time. "How d'you mean?"

"I mean, Mr. Leach, that you're behind the times." The warm-cold smile was offered again. "Warrick's out already."

Jesus.

"Oh, yes."

"I don't believe—"

"I've been told to keep my trap shut, but the information's cast-iron. The prodigal boy's come home, all right, Mr. Leach. Within the past twelve hours or so. They've got him shacked up near Tower Bridge under the name of Shepherd."

Dekker flipped his fingers. "North Tower, that's the place. They keep a debriefing pad there. . . . Pity you couldn't have beaten him to it. A week ago, say, and I'd really have taken you on."

25

The fear that clutched at Leach was like ice, terror in the chill of it, panic in its shocking thaw.

Warrick out.

A sickening despair eventually propelled him away from Dekker's flat. How long he stayed after Dekker dropped the bombshell he never knew, and what he said—if he uttered anything at all—he never remembered. But Dekker's voice seemed to go on and on, amiably regretful, taking up time, *time.*

"Bad luck, Mr. Leach. Afraid you just missed the boat."

Warrick out ... Out already.

The menace of it gripped Leach's heart, spun his mind. Each minute seemed a lifetime, and he thought Dekker would meander on forever.

"Traitor's an old-fashioned word these days, but that's what Warrick is. And it's my belief a good few people are going to wish he'd stayed where he was. Over at North Tower they'll pick him clean."

Leach got away at last, down the stairs three at a time, out to the street. There were no taxis. For precious minutes he frantically searched the oncoming traffic, then heard the rumbling clank-clank of an overhead train and sprinted for the nearby station.

Howard hadn't known about Warrick: two hours ago he hadn't known a thing. So when exactly had Warrick arrived? And what damage had he done already?

The questions raged as Leach ran. He missed the first train and caught the next, frantic at the short delay, feeling threatened all the time. "Deep water is for those who can swim, my friend"—Retman's words jabbed at him. Retman who'd failed to respond last night. Retman who'd been absent when it mattered most. Significantly absent.

Had *he* jumped the gun as well? Gone to ground? Lost his nerve?

Bastard, either way. Hybrid bastard.

At Earl's Court Leach changed trains, shouldering through the afternoon crowds. He was too far gone in desperation to sense the pressure of an unseen gaze, but at South Kensington he obeyed his instinct and left the train, side-stepping back in again when the doors were all but shut, doing it for safety's sake, the hunted feeling very strong, the sense of everything closing in.

Gray would have an answer.

He left the train a second time at Sloane Square and rode up to the surface on the escalator. There were taxis here and he got the first to come cruising by.

"Golden Jacey's, St. Martin's Lane."

"Righto, guv."

Twelve minutes to four.

Gray knew how to survive.

Shakily, Leach lit a cigarette, London going by. TOUCH-BUTTON CASUALTIES NOW TOTAL 500. He didn't want to see, scared out of his mind without that, the dream game turned to nightmare. All the time he felt that, no matter what he did, it was going to be too late.

Twice before, he had been to Golden Jacey's, reporting to Gray in the manner Warrick had instructed him, confirming the monthly delivery made to Nolan. Retman was a go-between, who paid him; and Nolan was a quartermaster, who supplied others. But Gray was a controller, who used what he was given. Leach had no illusions that weren't self-imposed. In his heart he knew, had always known. Gray was a linchpin operations executive for God knows what, and Warrick would name him quick as knife.

Leach sweated thinly. The taxi finished with the Mall and went under Admiralty Arch, worked clockwise around Trafalgar Square and swung left towards the Cavell Memorial.

Gray would know how to cope. *Had to know.* There was nowhere else to turn, no one else to warn. Leach crushed the half-smoked cigarette under his heel and lit another, hollows in his cheeks, eyes never still, whole worlds in them of loneliness and desperation.

Golden Jacey's had a garish stucco façade framed with ribbons of colored neon. Tourists came here, men without women, all sorts, six days a week, noon till midnight. The name was picked out in winking lights above the mirrored entrance. On either side of the box office were large photographs of a florid-faced, crinkle-haired man seated at a grand piano and wearing a huge-lapeled green velvet suit. On each of the display boards, jauntily lettered above the photograph, the passer-by could read:

GRAYTIME IS PLAYTIME

Below, more discreetly set out, the wording was:

JUST ASK GRAY
1400–1700 : 1800–2100

Leach checked the time as he quit the taxi. It was seven minutes after four. Beyond the box office the entrance funneled towards double doors. Leach pushed through into a dimly lit reception lobby, where a uniformed attendant exchanged his coat for a claim ticket. The rancid smell of damp hung in the warm enclosed air, and, above the whirring of an extractor fan, Leach could faintly hear the piano.

"D'you want any request discs?"

Yes, he wanted discs.

"How many, sir?" They were expensive.

"One."

There was a second door, THIS WAY TO GRAY hooped above the lintel. Leach crossed the lobby and opened the door and stepped through into another world.

Twice before, he'd been here, the initial effect the same

each time, eyes adjusting, everything a soft, soft pink, Gray at the piano on the low dais straight ahead and a couple of dozen tables grouped in a horseshoe pattern around a central floor area. There was a bar set back on the left amid murky pools of descended light. A naked blonde was on the dais as usual, reclining on a chaise lounge at the piano's waist: every half hour a different girl took over, but they were always blondes.

Gray was playing "Satisfy Me," busy with his flourishes, fingers flipping over the keys. Only about half of the tables were occupied, and Leach selected the vacant one at the middle of the horseshoe, everything so compact that even there he wasn't more than thirty feet from the piano. But Gray didn't see him, heavy shoulders shrugging as he played, foot pumping the pedals. Six hours a day he did this: the rest was striptease and so-called international cabaret.

Every table was fitted with a glass-domed slot machine at its center, the machine about the size of a coffeepot. Leach wasted no time. He inserted his metal request disc the moment he was seated. Immediately, the glass dome glowed and a crisp sheet of paper was ejected from the base. Immediately, too, the blonde rose languidly from where she reclined and started towards the signal.

A beam of tinted light shone down from the canopied ceiling and followed her across the dais. Her nakedness was startling under this sudden light. Her breasts were full and firm, the nipples quivering as she walked; and she walked with long, slow, model's stride, balanced on the highest of high heels and wearing nothing except a golden pouch slung like a sporran across the front of her on a tasseled rope of glittering beads.

That, and a smile.

Scores of eyes fingered her as she came across the floor to Leach's table, stepping into her own tight dark shadow as the spotlight followed and Gray played on.

159

Satisfy me, don't deny me
One more time . . .

JUST ASK GRAY was the heading on the square of paper, and JUST ASK GRAY was beaded on the girl's gold pouch. Leach scribbled something and folded the paper twice. Twice before he'd done the same—reporting a success and requesting a rendezvous: a mercenary, signing in. This time he wrote: *Warrick in London. Urgent we meet now, repeat now—Leach.*

Gray must tell him what to do, how to cope.

The blonde was almost at his table now, white thighs and hips and silvery-shadowed belly, the pouch provocatively and loosely slung. Leach glanced up at the mauve eyes and the smiling mouth that was redder than blood. She tossed her long blonde hair as she came to a halt in front of him, a foot away at most, the pointed breasts incredibly sensual in the angled light.

"Something for Gray?" she asked, soft and high-pitched.

Excite me, ignite me
One more time . . .

Leach reached for the pouch, untouched by lust as she slightly arched her back and smiled, inviting him, teasing with a forward twitch of her pelvis. He unclipped the flap and dropped the folded note inside the pouch, then fastened the clip again, needing both hands as he fumbled to make it fast. Farther around the horseshoe of tables someone laughed, phlegm curdling in the throat, and the blonde maintained the smile.

"Thank you, sir."

She turned and started back, tight buttocks, hips swaying, waist like an hourglass. Gray was coming to an end of "Satisfy Me." The blonde moved slowly, trapped magnificently in the whiteness of the splash of light, and every

160

head swiveled with her, every pair of eyes. She stepped onto the dais and curtsied towards Gray, then opened the pouch and placed the request note on a waiting salver.

The spotlight died. Everything was pink again, misty with cigarette smoke. Amid applause the girl subsided onto the chaise lounge and Gray finished playing. Leach watched him intently. The girl's perfume was around him still but he didn't notice it.

"Well, gentlemen." The felt-covered microphone quivered like a bulrush inches from Gray's twisted smile. "What's Gloria got for me this time? Sure brings the requests out of you fellows, Gloria does, a lot of which—well, sorry, but what kind of girl d'you figure she is? . . . Eh?"

He had a deep voice, nasal, easy-come-easy-go, and he used the selfsame patter week in and week out. He glanced around at the tables as he spoke, and when he spotted Leach he gave no sign of recognition. Just another customer with money to spend and his libido showing. But he picked up the request slip at once and began to open it.

"By the way, last night we had a character in who made out his request via one of the girls and asked: 'Do you happen to know her telephone number?' To which—you've guessed it—I said: 'If you can hum it, brother, I promise you—' "

He broke off, staring at what Leach had written. Whatever else, he could act. From the floor it genuinely looked as if he was stricken with sudden pain. Twice he made an effort to continue, anxious, it seemed, to read the request and go on. A murmur of concern came from the tables; the blonde by the piano rose uncertainly to her feet.

"Sorry," Gray managed. "I'm . . . very sorry, gentlemen—"

He lurched off the dais, one hand to his face, and vanished backstage. The girl went after him. Half a min-

161

ute later someone in shirt sleeves came on with a notice, which he propped against the microphone.

GRAY IS INDISPOSED

Taped music started coming through. The lights swelled up a shade. But Leach didn't wait. Once Gray made his move, he moved, too, quickly, slipping away with a terrible urgency, reaching for his coat ticket as he made for the exit.

"Now?" the Special Branch man with Howard whispered.

"Not yet. Give them a run."

Howard had arrived within minutes of getting the call. All eyes were on the girl when he sidled in, and his first temptation had been to intercept the message Leach sent up.

But no. Cat and mouse. He wanted more than this, and he could get it. Revenge was part of the reward.

"Let 'em go," he said, anonymous among the background shadows of the bar. "It's early yet."

They went out by a side door, push-bar into the street, the man with Howard struck by his calm. It was icy, unnatural; yet, within himself, Howard was exultant. The first hints of dusk were already in the air as they walked to the car and slammed themselves in and waited.

"They won't go far," Howard said, sure of everything suddenly, an unbelievable feeling after so much guesswork. "Tube station, public lavatory—that'll be the kind of place."

He started the engine as they listened to the first of Leach's tails reporting back on the walkie-talkie.

"Monmouth Street, still . . . Earlham Street . . . Charing Cross Road now, going north again . . ." Every half minute or so, brief and metallic-sounding. "Manette Street . . ."

The Special Branch man cocked his head. "Soho Square? What d'you bet?"

Howard grunted.

"Into Greek Street, continuing north . . ."

"You're right," Howard said.

He dropped into gear and released the brake. They started moving.

"Soho Square, the western side of Soho Square . . ." Switch off, switch on, fifteen seconds in between, a different man this time. "Gone into a Catholic Church at the corner of Sutton Row . . ."

Howard made Soho Square inside three minutes— throttle and brake and horn. He ran the car into an empty space a little way past the church and abandoned it there. His skin tingled as he walked the few yards back, the Special Branch man at his side.

Now, his mind throbbed. Now, after all this time.

He knew the church. Half of Soho's residents came here. Waiters, cooks, shopkeepers, prostitutes, croupiers— they came when they could, not always at the set times, lighting a candle and kneeling to pray, reverting to the language of their childhood, the broken and accented English of their trade not good enough to explain themselves to God.

Howard entered swiftly, grateful for the blue-and-gold gloom and the amount of tiptoed comings and goings. It was after five on a Friday evening and he was far from being alone.

One of the tails was waiting, browsing through some C.T.S. leaflets. "Second row back from the front."

Howard nodded. Up to a score of people were dotted unevenly about the pews, women mostly, but there was no mistaking Leach and Gray, despite Gray having slipped on an overcoat. Howard moved into a seat at the very back, and the Special Branch man went elsewhere. The stale

163

smell of incense was immensely strong and evocative; Howard's nostrils flared. His face was as hard as flint as he rested elbows on knees and waited, watching the agitated mime up front.

And it was good to watch; worth savoring. He'd come a long way for this.

Gray was the key now. Before it was dark his interrogation would have started—where? and when? and how? And who else? *Who else?* Within the hour the pressure would be on, and sooner or later Gray would open the doors that mattered.

Oh, yes.

Howard watched the heads close together, the urgent gesturing, enjoying the desperation he knew was there, crouched forward with his chin cupped in his hands while, in the painting above the altar, Christ looked down from the raised cross with the eyes of eternity. "All that love and pain," Harriet used to say. "Mercy is what the world needs most—don't you see? Don't you see?"

Against his will he remembered. The familiar was all around him and the smell of incense was heavy in his head, but he was out of lasting reach of the past. A multitude of human agonies, senseless and obscene, had taught him how to hate, and it was with hatred that he continued to wait and bide his time. Perhaps a quarter of an hour passed. The odd newcomer arrived—a man here, a woman there— and they blessed themselves, genuflected, bent their bodies. Howard was dead to that kind of belief, that kind of hope. He knew what he wanted, and it left no room for anything else.

Gray suddenly got to his feet, then Leach. They stood together, and from where Howard watched it looked as though they shook hands. He covered his face with his fingers and hunched his shoulders, tense again, flick-flick at the side of his mouth. He saw Leach nod. Then Gray turned away from him and started down the side aisle. The

164

Special Branch man got up as well—for all the world like someone who's prayed his heart out—and followed. They went outside within yards of each other. Gray going right, into Sutton Row.

He was picked up there almost immediately. No fuss, no disturbance. All the passers-by noticed were two men coming together in the street—as if for a light, or maybe for directions—and then some others converging, three at most; it was difficult to be sure. After which the squad car arrived.

Leach heard the squeal of tires while he was still inside, but he didn't associate it with himself. A couple of minutes after Gray's departure he also made a move, seemingly with reluctance, hands deep in his pockets, hugging his coat about him. A permanent state of faded daylight filled the church, and though he passed quite close to where Howard knelt, Howard had no qualms. In years to come he was to remember the fleeting glimpse he had of Leach's face as he walked by: through meshed fingers it looked as though he was in a kind of stupor.

Howard gave him time to get clear of Soho Square. Then he came out into the real autumnal dusk and went at the double to where the Granada was slewed with two wheels up on the pavement.

Fear had brought Leach this far. Greed had put its hooks into him, back in the summer, but fear was the lever now, and fear would take him where Howard expected him to go. In his bones he knew it: once a puppet always a puppet. Gray was taken care of, but Leach he wanted for himself.

26

Leach had never seen North Tower before. When he was last in the vicinity of the Tower of London he had been a mere boy and the riverside apartment block wasn't even there. He stared at it now with dread in his heart. Others dealt with death at first hand: others killed. He wasn't ready for what had to be done in order to survive.

"No," he'd protested to Gray. "Not me. Jesus, not me."

"You," Gray said stonily. "It's got to be you. There's two or three I can call on, but they've all gone north and I couldn't raise them before tomorrow. And tomorrow'll be too late."

Neither had Leach ever touched a gun before. It was small and solid and awful to hold, yet it could save him. He understood that. How else was Warrick to be silenced? He accepted that, nothing real any more.

"Good man," Gray had said, urgent with praise at the moment of parting. "Good man, y'are."

Leach couldn't move his mind from his fear. The pressure of what he had come to do was like a sickness, gnawing at him, eating away what remained of his sanity. In the enveloping silence of the church, whispering tersely together he had seen Gray's dismay turn into panic and from panic into chilling decision. Ever since he had learned about Warrick from Dekker he had told himself that Gray would have a solution, suggest a way, but never once had it occurred to him that this might be it.

Others know how to kill. Not him. But action was essential, immediate action, before everyone went to the wall. Gray's eyes had burned into his. The longer the delay the less the chance of success.

"You . . . It's got to be you."

The taxi U-turned and rattled away towards Tower Hill:

Leach half listened to it going while he stared up at the building he was about to enter. Twenty stories high, white stone and fawn-tinted glass. Warrick was in there somewhere, Warrick who had dazzled him with money out in the open on an alien summer's day and who now had run for safety and expected quarter, offering names as bribes to earn himself merit.

"Over at North Tower they'll pick him clean. . . ."

Leach crossed to the entrance, NORTH TOWER gilded in marble slabs on either side of the huge glass double doors. The doors closed with a soft squeeze of air after he'd gone through. Inside he glanced about him, the carpeted silence unnerving, no one there, no one in the porter's office cubicle, not even the sound of himself as he moved.

To the side of the cubicle was a plate with name cards and apartment numbers. Leach ran a finger down the cards, checking. Shepherd was the name Dekker had said Warrick was using, and sure enough there was a Shepherd listed against Number 58. Something coiled itself in his stomach when he saw it: the card was new, the name written in ink instead of being printed, like the rest, suggesting Warrick had only recently arrived. From Lisbon. Overnight, probably; today even. In any event, recently enough for Howard not to have known about it only hours ago.

Leach straightened up, dry in the mouth, his nerves raw. Number 58 was on the fourteenth floor; but who was there besides Warrick? No one, Dekker had suggested. Just Warrick. "Tomorow'll be a different story. But for what's left of today I reckon they'll give him time to lick his wounds and sort himself out. Bound to."

He'd been so sure, so confident, everything that Leach was not. Leach stood in the lobby, close to the lifts, trying to prepare himself, sweat on the palms of his hands. This was nightmare. Incredibly, he had come to kill. It was essential, vital; the whole of his future hung on it, his life

with Anna, the escape they had planned. The fear of failure swept through him again, more powerful than the fear
of the act itself.

He didn't know how to kill: but he would because he
must.

A numbness grew in his brain, yet his heart was pounding. There were three lifts and he took the nearest one—
no more than eight persons, mahogany veneer, maker's
name, telephone; with heightened awareness he noticed.
An approaching sound made him jab the fourteenth-floor
button, a panic never far away, scared in case he was seen
or someone came to ride up with him.

The doors trundled across. With a dull whine the lift
began to move and the floor lights started flashing on and
off. Leach's right hand tightened around the butt of the
pistol, unreal, unreal, all of this, a weakness taking him in
his legs. Suddenly he couldn't remember what Warrick
looked like, couldn't believe that fear would be enough.

He took the safety catch off the gun in the way Gray
had quickly showed him. In the instant that he did it the
lift jerked to a standstill. No warning. One moment it was
rising normally, the next there was a jarring thud and
Leach staggered: in the sudden silence he could hear the
cables vibrating in the shaft above and below. He shot a
glance at the floor-indicator panel, but none of the lights
was showing.

Six? Seven?

He pressed the button for the fourteenth floor, but
nothing happened. He wasn't really alarmed, not even
then. Twice more he pressed the same button, then tried
others at random, up and down the panel. The lift didn't
budge. He swore, a little more frantic, and put sideways
pressure on the door with the flat of his hands in case a
circuit had been broken, contact not made; but the lift
stayed put.

Disaster was on him already, and a part of him knew it.

168

Chance had sprung a trap, brought everything to an abrupt end. He knew it even as he flicked the buttons all over again from top to bottom, muttering, sweat beginning to stream.

In desperation he snatched up the telephone. There was no dial. He rattled the rest furiously to attract the porter.

BREAKDOWN INSTRUCTIONS
LIFT RECEIVER AND WAIT

He read as he waited, licked his lips, shifted his stance, despair mounting all the time. Nothing happened, no one answered. He kept bouncing the rest, getting a dry click-click-click. A vein had swollen in his forehead, like a fat worm beneath the skin.

"Yes?" a voice said at last.

"Get me down."

"I don't think I know how to do that."

"Then call the porter, for Christ's sake."

"I'll do that presently, Leach."

Leach?

Leach?

He caught his breath, shaken, incredulous. "Who's there? . . . Who's there?" he repeated, tossed on a frightened wave of stupefaction. And his scalp seemed to shrink as the answer came.

"It's Howard, Leach. Duncan Howard."

For a terrified moment Leach felt as if he were falling. He couldn't speak. Time seemed to lose its shape, alarm rampaging behind the trauma.

"Come to visit your friend, have you?"

"I don't understand."

"Warrick . . . Your friend Warrick."

"What are you trying to say?"

"I've done with playing games, that's what."

Leach stalled, desperate to gain a little time. Shock was in his eyes. "Get me down, will you?"

"Later."

"There's no air in this place, and I can't stand being—"

"Later." A moment's silence. "It's over, Leach. Finished."

"What d'you mean?"

"From now on it's you and me. Just you and me."

Sweat splashed on the lift floor. Out of an appalled confusion Leach managed not to falter. "I went to see Dekker for you." They'd been allies, the tone stressed. "I showed him the photograph and told him what you wanted, exactly what you wanted."

"Yes?"

"And he said Warrick was already out. . . . He said he was here."

"Then he lied to you."

"At North Tower. Under the name of Shepherd. That's why—"

"He lied to you. He was asked to lie to you."

"Dekker?"

"We've all lied to you, Leach."

The silence then was longer than the last. "How?" Leach heard himself fumble. "In what way?"

"Wherever Warrick happens to be, it isn't here."

"In Lisbon, then?" He still couldn't swallow what had been done to him; not quite. "Is that what you're telling me?"

"Warrick was never in Lisbon," Howard grated. "Not to my knowledge."

"But yesterday, in Warsaw, you stated as a known fact—"

"I was using you, Leach. I wanted to see where you'd go when we got to London."

"I went to Dekker. Where you asked me to go."

"After Dekker."

Howard waited, alone in the porter's cubicle, destructive power in every second he held back.

"*After* Dekker, Leach. And you obliged. You gave us Gray like a gift."

"Let me down," Leach said weakly. "There are things I have to tell you."

"Later." Then Howard jeered: "How was Warrick to be killed?"

No answer.

"Did Gray give you a gun? Or did you bring a Touchbutton of your own?"

No answer.

"You ought to be good at killing. You've done enough of it."

"Let me down," Leach pleaded, knuckle bones white through the skin. "For God's sake. You've got me wrong, all wrong. . . . I swear to you. There's been a crazy misunderstanding."

"Listen," Howard snapped. "Listen, or I'll pull the plug on the lift and you'll drop like a stone. There was a headline today—five hundred Touchbutton victims, that's what it said. Five hundred, Leach. Yours, all of 'em yours." His voice frayed, deep in the throat.

"No . . . No."

"Some of them I saw. Those on the ferryboat, for instance. I saw what you did there—the maimed and the blinded as well as the dead, the women and kids as well as the troops."

"I was never told what I carried."

"But you knew. Jesus Christ, you knew."

Leach pressed his forehead against the smooth side of the lift. "When I met Warrick—"

"When you met Warrick you agreed to carry a weapon that blew a friend of mine and a colleague of mine to pieces. Plus all the others." Howard spat it out. "You came too near to home, Leach. What's happening now is private, something personal in return."

171

"I can explain."

"Explain?" Through the window of the porter's cubicle Tower Bridge could be seen, its dark bulk picked out in lights. *"Explain?"*

"You don't understand. I had finished with those people."

"You?"

"It was over. As far as I was concerned it was over. All right, I knew what the loads were—though not to begin with. I didn't realize then. But as soon as it became obvious—"

Leach broke off: one of the other lifts had started moving. He listened to the droning hum and the faint sound of someone getting in or out. It made him stab the buttons again, wildness in his eyes, trapped in more ways than one. The sweaty silence returned, undermining him a shade more.

"Let me down," he said.

"When I've done with you." Howard's voice was like a whip. "Then you're welcome."

Leach blinked his stinging eyes. He stumbled into a reiteration of his ignorance—"It was all a mistake, a terrible mistake"—mentioning regret, horror, hoping as he did so that Howard even now might soften enough to open the doors and let him out.

"You don't seem to understand. I'd finished with them. That's what I went to tell Gray."

But Howard said: "You'd given an undertaking to make ten deliveries, and the most you tried to do was duck out of your obligation for one month only."

No answer.

"Fifty Touchbuttons every month, from August last to May next."

"It was a mistake, I tell you. Hell, I represent a leading international company in that area of Europe, and it would have been madness, out and out madness—"

"To run something on the side?"

"I didn't realize they were weapons."

172

"A thousand pounds a month and you didn't realize what you were handling? That day at Galatorsko and you didn't ask? Those shipments out of Rotterdam, with Ireland as a destination, and you didn't put two and two together?" With savage scorn Howard said: "Am I a child, d'you think?"

No answer, seconds ticking away.

"You hadn't finished with them, Leach. A month's postponement was the most you ever asked for."

"Did Retman tell you that?"

"Retman?" Howard countered.

"You prefer his word to mine?" Leach was beside himself, guessing and guessing wrong. "I don't know what he's been telling you—"

"Retman—whoever Retman is—has told me nothing. . . . Nothing, d'you hear?"

"Then how can you pretend—?"

Leach dried there, and to Howard it seemed almost as if he was too petrified to go any further, suddenly aware of some alternative he had never contemplated.

"You told me yourself, Leach."

"Never!"

"You, yes. Every word."

"That's impossible."

"Listen, if you don't believe me."

Howard had brought a pocket casette player with him. Twice his mouth pulled sideways as he placed the telephone close by the speaker. Red-eyed and pitiless he started the tape running—last night's tape, which Petrie had dispatched from Warsaw by a later plane. It hadn't been in London for two hours yet.

"Listen to this, Leach."

"*How much are you paid?*"

"*A thousand pounds. Each time a thousand pounds.*"

"*And what do you carry?*"

"*Radio equipment.*"

173

"And you take this radio equipment from Poland?"

"Leipzig . . . Poland has nothing to do with it."

"In the trailer?"

"That's right."

"To Ireland?"

"Transshipped out of Rotterdam . . . I undertook to carry ten consignments. What I've been trying to do is to persuade them to release me from making a delivery next month. . . . So that there would be room for you."

"And they said no?"

"They said no."

Howard stopped the tape and picked up the telephone.

"Leach? . . . There's more if you want to hear."

Leach's face was ashen, his eyes wide in a blaze of dismay. "How did you get hold of that?"

"With the lady's help."

"No!"

"The answer's yes."

"I don't believe you." He shouted, shaking now, losing the control he had clung to for so long. Memories of Anna seared his mind. "She wouldn't have helped *you*. That's madness. Oh, Christ, that can't be true. . . ."

"She lied to you."

In desperation Leach said: "You're bluffing."

"The bluffing's finished with. And the lying. We all lied to you, Leach, but Anna Dabrowska lied best and most of all."

Howard ran the tape again, brutally, malice like an acid in the darkness of his heart, the desire for revenge overpowering.

"I love you, Martin."

"Keep telling me that."

"Always . . . Always, don't worry."

"I need you, Anna."

"Martin . . ."

"Yes?"

174

"Come back tomorrow night. Don't stay over there. . . ."

Howard cut the tape. He could hear Leach's breathing.

"You're an amateur, Leach. You always were. But Anna Dabrowska's an out-and-out pro—one of the best we have over there."

There was sobbing now, and a frenzied hammering of fists, followed by quiet.

Then Howard heard the sudden bark of the gun and knew it was all over.

It was ten minutes before he was able to restore the fuses and have the lift brought down. An ambulance was on its way by then, and as the doors of the lift slid open he could hear the high-low siren of an approaching police car.

He gazed down at Leach with what remained of his hatred. And what struck him most was how quickly death could transform the weaknesses printed on a living face into a look of innocence.

≋ **27**

Howard drove home to Kingston Hill: home is the place where you have to go. It was nine o'clock by the time the Granada powered up the last long rise, five minutes past as he swung into the driveway with a crunching of gravel.

The square house looked cheerless and deserted. No lights were showing, and Eve's Mini wasn't in the garage. He heaved himself out from behind the wheel, weary from what now seemed an everlasting day: he felt empty, completely drained. "There are all manner of betrayals,

Leach"—one of his taunts haunted him still and wouldn't let go. Somewhere along the way he'd supposed revenge would bring about fulfillment; but there wasn't any. A devil had gone out of him and nothing had taken its place, nothing but exhaustion, limp and leaden-eyed.

"Eve?"

He called as he entered the house from the garage, switching on lights as he went, knowing she wasn't sitting somewhere in the dark yet calling her name just the same: only death is not a habit.

"Eve?"

He crossed the sitting room's soft wall-to-wall pile and poured himself a gigantic Scotch. No ice, no water, too flaked-out to bother, but needing the whiskey, wincing at its stiffening after-bite. He had somehow expected a greeting, but how still the house was, and how lonely. It was anticlimax to come home and find nobody with whom to share a success, something on the Touchbutton credit side at last yet no one to tell. "Congratulations," the Home Secretary had phoned about Gray. "Good work, Howard."

But here, no one and nothing.

Howard looked at the cards lined along the mantelpiece and tried to tell himself that Eve's birthday had come and gone only days before. The roses were still in the hall, and yet it might have been weeks ago, months even. And the cards seemed to be from strangers, names he couldn't fit to faces.

He must have glanced at the envelope with his own name on it at least three times before the penny dropped and he took it down. Eve wasn't one for leaving notes around for him to find and its discovery surprised him. He slit the envelope open and read.

Dear Duncan,
I think it's better if I go away, at least for a while.
Don't start ringing people round; I won't be with friends

or anywhere I'm known, so spare yourself—and me—that embarrassment.

With disbelief Howard read on.

Having trusted and respected each other enough to make a life together it's awful when something happens to change the way things were. What that something is in our case I can't exactly say, but it's as if a part of you had begun to die or was always somewhere else.

Forgive me. When I first met you I remember being told by people who knew her that Harriet was a very special kind of person. None of the words we use is any good, but tenderness was one of her qualities, I believe, and concern, as well as ability to share her love with those who needed it most.

I need these things from you, Duncan. Since before Touchbutton started I've needed them, so it isn't just that to blame.

Eve

Howard crumpled the note with a squeeze of his hand. A sense of shock and bitter hurt burst deep inside him, like a voice crying aloud. For a long moment he didn't seem capable of moving, no volition, all power of decision gone. But presently he drank, emptying his glass with a nervous backward toss of the head, and went to the decanter for more.

Yesterday, she'd written it yesterday, after he'd left for Warsaw.

. . . better if I go away, at least for a while.

He dwelt on that. In the mirror above the abandoned birthday cards he looked at himself, tired and bewildered now, yet aware—because he searched for it—of a hardness in the eyes and a severity in the set of the face that revenge should have wiped away.

177

"Eve," he said to the room. "Oh God, Eve."

He drew a quick shallow breath and turned his back on his reflection. It was no time to be accused, to feel found out: all manner of emotions took their turn, guilt among them. The crumpled paper slipped from his hand, but what Eve had written kept him in turmoil.

He wasn't sure about himself any more. "Leach" was all he seemed to hear. "Listen, Leach"—his own voice, on and on, merciless and unrelenting. "We led you by the nose, Leach. . . ." A bully's voice, vindictive and obsessed.

Yet triumphant, that at least: justified. "Congratulations . . . Good work, Howard."

He went into the kitchen, past the roses Sheard had arranged for Eve to receive, the sense of loss wrung out of him. When he found himself in the kitchen he couldn't think why he was there and he went back into the sitting room, restless and uncertain, wretched with the sum of separate hurts and longings. The sins of omission were the hardest to bear.

. . . at least for a while.

He read into it all he could, listening to his thoughts. He sipped the whiskey. Just then he thought he heard the sound of a car, but dismissed it as imagination. The house seemed more than merely quiet; it was dead. And he suddenly felt weary beyond all things because he seemed to understand none of them.

The doorbell chimed, and hope flickered revealingly. He checked his watch as he hurried into the hall: nine-twenty-five.

"Good evening, Mr. Howard." It was Vaughan.

"Why, hello." Howard stamped the disappointment down. "Come in, come in."

"I'm sorry to call at this time of night—"

"Not at all."

"—but you left your bag at the office, and I know what

178

it's like if you find yourself stuck in the morning without a razor or something."

"It could have waited," Howard said. "I'd have managed, but thanks all the same. You've come a long way off course."

"As it happens, I'm on my way home, sir."

"Oh? Where d'you live, then?"

"Richmond."

"I didn't know."

So much he didn't know, about others and about himself. "What'll you drink? . . . Scotch?"

"With dry ginger, please." Then Vaughan said: "Have you any later news on tonight's Touchbutton?"

Howard straightened, turning. "*Tonight's?*"

"In Leicester Square, sir."

"Tell me."

"The film première there."

Howard shook his head. "I hadn't heard."

"Nine o'clock BBC reported it as the worst yet—over two hundred casualties."

Howard ran a hand over his face as if to hide the insistent sidelong flick of his mouth. "I didn't realize they were weapons." Another voice shook in his mind for an instant; Leach was on the dark end of it. To have nursed thoughts of triumph was madly premature: this war, this murderous war, had far from run its course.

He heard Vaughan saying: "How many Touchbuttons do we reckon C.I.V.A. have at their disposal?"

"Three batches of fifty. Minus what they've put to use already."

"Which means there's an awful long way to go."

It was a statement. Vaughan took the proffered tumbler as Howard said stiffly: "We've blocked one source of supply and we're in the process of cracking one major cell. That's quite a start, quite a breakthrough."

"But they'll form others, surely?"

"Probably."

"Find other carriers?"

"Probably."

Howard didn't want to contemplate the future: the past had cost him enough as it was. "Leach? . . . Leach?" With awful clarity he could still recall his hatred and how he'd squeezed it out like pus. And the way he'd used Anna Dabrowska in the manner a pimp employs a whore; for gain. And the lies and the deceits and Leach's heartbreak worked for and achieved at the very end.

He didn't like what he'd become. He told himself this, over and over, and frightened himself with the thought of the pressures still in store and what they might do to him yet. The longer Touchbutton's bloody road went on the more it would corrupt him. No need for other Chisholms, other Sheards; he could go on hating without them. Colin had seen the signs and told him so.

"It's unfair to Eve, the way you are. . . ."

Eve, he protested silently, hands clenched at his side, jealous of her youth and beauty, aware only now that here was the mainspring of much of his malice. Eve, he thought. Eve, for God's sake.

Home was the place where they had to take you in.

I need you, too, Eve. I need help.

To Vaughan he said: "Excuse me," and crossed the room to the telephone. It was vital he speak to the Home Secretary about Leicester Square. "Mercy is what the world needs most"—even then he remembered, and he thought: Sure, sure. So let someone else start using it.

He paused, about to dial, the receiver lifted off the rest. "How old are you, Vaughan?"

"Twenty-seven."

"And you've been in the department—?"

"Four months."

"Four months." Howard nodded, thinking back, thinking

forward, something learned but not enough. "Want my advice?"

"Sir?"

"Get out," he said to the youthful, earnest, uncomprehending face. "Get out while the going's good. Before it's too late. While you're still what you are."